Me
and
Brenda

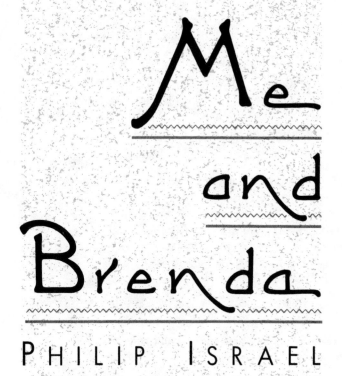

Me
and
Brenda

PHILIP ISRAEL

W · W · Norton & Company
New York · London

Printed in the United States of America.

The text of this book is composed in 11/14
Compano, with the display set in Greeting
Monotone. Composition and manufacturing by
The Haddon Craftsmen, Inc. Book design by
Guenet Abraham.

First Edition.

Library of Congress Cataloging-in-Publication
Data

Israel, Philip.
   Me and Brenda / Philip Israel.
      p. cm.
   I. Title.
PS3559.S75M4   1990
813'.54—dc20   89-29477

ISBN 0-393-02860-7

W.W. Norton & Company, Inc., 500 Fifth Avenue,
New York, N.Y. 10110
W.W. Norton & Company, Ltd., 37 Great Russell
Street, London WC1B 3NU
1 2 3 4 5 6 7 8 9 0

For Lenore

Me
and
Brenda

1

ONE DAY I GET A CALL TO PICK UP A CUSTOMER IN
front of the Green Leaf Tavern in Woodside. I pull up there, the guy gets in the back
seat but instead of telling me where he
wants to go he leans over to the front, puts
out his hand, and says to me, "Croppe. Al
Croppe. C-r-o-p-p-e."

Now I'm in that cab to make money, not
tell people if they're acting strange or not, so
I shake his hand and tell him it's a pleasure
to have him in my car. He gives me an address in Manhattan and I start heading for
the Queensborough Bridge. He turns out to
be a talker. He goes on and on but I'm

hardly paying attention. While we're on the bridge he says, "Sid General wants me to do the sheets." At that time I never heard of Sid General and for all I knew he was talking about laundry. He says, "It's a lot of work when I do the sheets but I pick winners nine out of ten times. You know anybody who can pick winners nine out of ten times?"

I say, "No sir! Nine out of ten! That's amazing!"

I get a lot of passengers who know how to pick winners but none of them are dressed too good.

A couple of days later, after my shift, I'm sitting in the Green Leaf Tavern and a guy comes up to me and says, "Rabbit Ears." I look at him like he's nuts. He says, "Third race. Aqueduct. I did the sheets today."

When I finished eating I walked over to the OTB office which is only two doors down from the Green Leaf Tavern. I put five dollars on Rabbit Ears to win. I'm not a gambler but I don't ignore a tip that drops on me from out of nowhere like that. The next day Rabbit Ears paid me fifty-five dollars.

Subsequently, Max, the afternoon bartender at the Green Leaf, told me something about this guy Croppe. There's a twenty-four-hour-a-day, seven-day-a-week poker game at Sid General's apartment, which is somewhere in the neighborhood, and this guy Croppe plays once a week, usually on Friday. He'll start at two or three in the morning and play till afternoon, twelve hours at a time, then he'll come into the Green Leaf for breakfast.

Now, I spend some time in the Green Leaf myself, and I happen to be the type of person who gets along with all kinds of people. So, you sit in the Green Leaf, you have a few beers and people get to talking. If you sit long enough you hear everything, and you hear everybody's version of it.

The Green Leaf is located in Woodside, at the intersection of Roosevelt and Broadway. I call this area Woodside but some people say it's Jackson Heights. There's no official boundary so you can call it what you want. But I'll admit one thing—Woodside is the wrong type of name for this area. There are no woods around here. It is not, as they say out west, Big Sky country. What we got here are buildings. Not like in Manhattan but still pretty big. You could say that this area is a city in its own right. We got thousands of houses, dozens, maybe hundreds, of ten- to twenty-story apartment buildings, stores, restaurants, law offices, gas stations, you name it. We got a big hospital, Elmhurst General, a few blocks down. And there are all kinds of people living around here—Irish, Hungarians, Jewish, Korean, Chinese, Indian, Colombian—you name it, we got it. We also got the IRT subway running overhead on Roosevelt Avenue. We got the IND subway running under Broadway. We got a station overhead for the IRT which is built right over the street with stairs going up and down and more stairs to the IND which has a station underground. So it's a very active place. We got more cars, trucks, buses, and people—more action crossing the intersection of Roosevelt and Broadway—than they got in the whole states of Wyoming, Colorado, and Montana put together.

I don't claim that this is the cleanest or the quietest place in the world. With all those steel girders from the Els we got plenty of pigeons overhead. I don't have to tell you what that means if you're walking underneath. But even so, this is a very nice place. In fact, if you take the time to look at it—and not many people do—but if you do, it's very impressive.

One day, about ten years ago, we had a blizzard. The wind was blowing and it snowed so hard you couldn't see five feet in front of you. I didn't work that day. I got up at five o'clock, which I always do, and it wasn't snowing yet. But I listened to the weather forecast, which was a lot different that morning than what I heard the night before. The night before they were saying, "No snow." It was supposed to snow south of here in Baltimore, Washington, maybe Philly, but not here. But at 5 A.M. they were saying it was going to be a big storm—twelve to fourteen inches. When I heard that I went back to bed. I was not going to get in a car and get stuck out on some side street or up on a bridge somewhere. One four-dollar ride could hang you up all day. A lot of people stayed home. The Green Leaf Tavern was open because Max and Genelli came in. They had no customers. All day long Max was wiping the bar, wiping the glasses, and looking out the window, which is not a bad way to earn a day's pay. Genelli, the cook, was sitting at a table in the back reading yesterday's paper, which is another good day's pay. Then, around two o'clock in the afternoon, Dave Winger came in.

Dave Winger first came to the Green Leaf about three or four months before that blizzard. When I saw him in there—and I'm not talking about the day of the blizzard now, because I wasn't there that day, I'm talking about the time three or four months before that, when I first laid eyes on him—I could see that he looked out of place. He was a young guy, twenty-three or twenty-four years old, and he didn't fit in. So naturally I went over and talked to him and after that we got friendly. But I'll get to his story later. Right now I'm talking about the day of the blizzard. At that time Dave was working all around this whole area—Woodside, Elmhurst, Maspeth, Jackson Heights—and when he got paid he'd walk over to the Green Leaf.

On the day of the blizzard he walked over from Elmhurst. He looked like a snowman when he came in. He orders a beer and he's about to order a plate of manicotti when all of a sudden the door blows open and in comes another snowman. This snowman slams the door shut and starts stamping his feet. He's wearing a fur coat and a fur hat and a big scarf, which he takes off and hangs up. This is Al Croppe. He's dressed like a college professor—tweed jacket with elbow patches, blue shirt, and a striped tie. And he starts right in. He says, "Max, we should work for the post office. Snow, sleet, nor rain will keep these harbingers from their appointed rounds. Gimme a hot drink, Max. Coffee Royale. This is a day that will live in infamy. It's gonna be remembered like the Blizzard of '88. You remember the old-timers talking about the Blizzard of '88? That's what we got here. A day that reminds me of poetry. I'm serious. Did I ever tell you that once upon a time I wanted to be a poet? If things were different, a little change of circumstances here or there, I could be in a loft in Soho right now writing poetry. You remember *Snowbound*? James Whitcomb Riley. When I was a

kid I memorized that poem. They had a two-day snowstorm
and this kid wakes up and looks out the window and he
says—

> "And when the second morning shone,
> We looked upon a world unknown.

"That line used to give me the chills. A world unknown.
Take a look out the window. Does that describe it or not? A
world unknown. You remember Miss Martin? We had her
in eleventh grade. Red eyes like she was always crying.
Thanatopsis by Walt Whitman:

> "Yet a few days,
> And the all-beholding sun
> Shall no more see thy corpse."

Then all of a sudden, in the middle of this, he turns
around to Winger and says, "Hey, guy, how about this
snow, huh? Al Croppe. C-r-o-p-p-e. Croppe." And he puts
out his hand.

Winger shakes hands and tells him his name.

Croppe says, "Whatta you drinkin'? Beer? It's eighteen
degrees Fahrenheit out there. This is no day for beer. You
got pipes inside. Intestines. That's like plumbing. It'll freeze
on a day like this. Give the man a hot drink, Max. Coffee
Royale for Mr. Winger and another one for me."

Dave says, "No thanks," but Max puts two cups up on the
bar, puts a big shot of booze in each one, and fills them with
hot coffee.

Croppe says, "To your health," and he takes a nice long sip. "Ahhhhhhh!" he says. "That's good! Feel that inside? Max, I been up all night. Real estate deal. Twenty-four million dollars. Lawyers from five firms sitting at the table. So much money on the line you couldn't blink an eye. Everybody figuring percentages. One fraction of a percent comes to hundreds of thousands of dollars. Lawyers like vultures. Agents. Salesmen. Each man for himself. You can't trust anybody. You can't blink an eye, Max."

Max is nodding. He's wiping the bar. He don't blink an eye. But he don't miss a word either. I know that because he's the one who told me what happened that day. First I got the story from Max and later I heard it from Dave.

Croppe says to Dave, "You look like a businessman yourself. Let me take a guess. I say you're a plumber. Am I right? You know why I guess that? Because every plumber I know dresses like he got his clothes in the Salvation Army. That's not an insult. Don't be insulted. To me, clothes mean nothing. I look in a guy's eyes. I look in his face. His phisonogomy. I'm looking at you right now and I say you have a very impressive face. I mean it. You're a guy that could command troops. I'm not kidding. I know people and I say you are a young man who could be very successful. You make a decision and you stick to it come hell or high water. Am I right? You're not taking me serious but I mean it. Max, tell him. I'm a businessman, Mr. Winger. I'm what is called an entrepen-ewer. My livelihood depends on knowing people. And I don't mean making their acquaintance. I mean judging them. Knowing what they're made of. I look at you and I see a young guy with potential. I look at you and I like what I see. Max, what's Mr. Winger's line of work? Plumbing?"

Max says, "He does everything. Plumbing, electrical, you name it. He's got a big reputation. I take his calls. You got a call from a lady in Maspeth today, Dave. Name is Della-wood. I got the number here. This guy has customers all over."

Al says, "Did I say it? I said it just from looking at his face."

Max says, "Some of these people think he's a saint."

"A saint?" Croppe says. "What's he do that makes him a saint?"

"He does good work," Max says.

Croppe looks from Max to Dave and back to Max. He doesn't believe this. He says, "Come on! Why is this guy a saint?"

Max says, "I didn't say he's a saint. They say it. One lady said it."

Croppe says, "You said he's a saint. You said, 'The man is a saint.' "

Max says, "Dave, tell him."

Dave is not going to get into this. He's got nothing to say.

So Max says, "He's a nice guy, he gives good prices, he treats people nice, he does extras for them, so they like him. Some of the people around here—you know the old people around here—the last time they had work done was twenty years ago. They call in somebody for an estimate and they can't believe what they hear so when they ask Dave he sounds cheap. And they all tell me he does beautiful work. So they love him."

Croppe says, "So the man is a saint because he gives a discount. Is that it? Okay. That's all right. I appreciate that. I understand it. As a matter of fact, I think it's good. There's a profit in that. But I don't understand why you get your calls here. Don't you have a phone?"

Dave doesn't answer.

Al says, "Max, doesn't he have a phone?"

Max says, "I guess not."

Al says, "He can't afford a phone?" Nobody answers. Al says, "That's okay. Nothing to be ashamed of. A lot of people can't afford phones. Listen, Dave, maybe we can help each other out. Tell me exactly what you do. You do painting?"

Dave nods.

"Carpenter? You also a carpenter?"

Dave nods.

"Electrical? You do electrical?"

He nods again. But he's not enjoying this.

Croppe says, "Jack-of-all-trades and you don't charge."

Dave says, "Of course I charge."

Croppe says, "But you work cheap. That's why you can't afford a phone. That's why you buy your clothes in the Salvation Army."

Dave says, "I don't buy my clothes in the Salvation Army."

Croppe says, "I know you don't. I just say that because it looks that way. Tell me, how do people hear about you?"

Dave says, "I don't know."

Croppe looks at Max. Max shrugs. He wants out of this

too. But Al says, "Max, how come they call here? How come you get so many phone calls?"

Max says, "I don't know. Word of mouth."

Croppe says, "Word of mouth? They call a bar? Would you hire a guy to fix your house by calling a bar?"

Max says, "Why not? The lady from Maspeth, the one I just said about, she heard from the lady in Elmhurst where he's workin' this week, Mrs. Blitnis."

Croppe says, "What's he doing for Mrs. Blitnis in Elmhurst?"

Max says, "Paintin' an apartment. And she heard about him from somebody else."

Croppe says, "Dave, I like what I hear. I got a proposition for you. Wait a minute! Let me talk. You haven't heard what I'm going to say."

Dave says, "I don't need to."

Croppe says, "I'm going to set you up in business—full backing—money to advertise, hire help, whatever you need. 'David Winger Home Repair.' How's that sound? And it's your business. You're in charge, not me. You price the jobs, you supervise the work, you hire the secretary. All I do is back you. Don't shake your head. I know what I'm talking about. Max, tell him. I'm a businessman. I'm what is called an entrepen-ewer. I put up the cash, you put up the know-how. That's all it takes. You start small but you grow big. You understand?" He takes out his checkbook and he waves it at Winger. "I got the cash right here," he says.

Dave says, "Forget it."

Croppe says, "Whatever you need. Just give me the number and I write it. Fifty thou? A hundred thou? You got it. Take the money, rent an office, hire a secretary, hire guys to do the work, and start advertising. 'Need a paint job? House look shabby? Call David Winger. David Winger will personally come to your house and discuss the job. No obligation. He'll make your house the showplace of the neighborhood.' We put it on billboards, newspapers, radio talk shows. The next thing you know people start to call. The secretary makes an appointment and you go see the job. You dress like an engineer. Safari outfit—pith helmet, khaki pants, khaki shirt, loops and pockets all over. You got stuff hanging from every loop. Measuring tape, pens, pencils, flashlight, clipboard. You name it. You rent a jeep. You drive to the house. 'Hi, I'm David Winger'—the Boss himself— 'We'll take care of everything. No problem.' And everybody gets a discount. That's what people want. Something for nothing. You take out your calculator. You figure you need two thousand dollars for this job. You put two thousand on the calculator and add maybe twenty-five percent. What's that come to? Twenty-five hundred. Am I right? Then you give 'em a discount. You split the difference. You say, 'That job would normally cost twenty-five hundred dollars but the price to you, with my Senior Citizen discount, is twenty-two fifty.' If they're not senior citizens, you've got a New Homeowners discount. If they're not new homeowners, you got a Washington's Birthday discount. If it's not Washington's Birthday, you got a Veteran's Day discount. You got a Spring Cleaning discount, a Fall Clearance discount, a Winter Snowball discount, a Summer Vacation discount. You

got a discount for everything and everybody. On top of that
you got freebies. You look over the job and you say, 'We're
doing so much for you here, why don't we really finish it up.
We're going to carpet those stairs for you for free. My gift to
you.' That's how you do business. You give things away.
You understand me? Now, you want to know why I'm doing
this. What's in it for me? Why am I being so generous? Well
I'm going to lay it on the line. I'm not being generous. I'm an
investor. I am what is called an entrepen-ewer. I look for
deals like this. I do deals like this every day. Tell him, Max.
Every day. The way it works, the standard form is, I get you
started, you cut me in on forty-nine percent and after the
business becomes successful you buy me out. We agree on a
price ahead of time. It's all put in writing. Legal. Black and
white. You're covered. I'm covered. And that's it. That's the
whole story. All I need from you is a figure." And he's waving his checkbook. "Name a figure and I make out the check
right now."

Dave says, "Max, who is this guy?"

Al says, "You don't like it? Is that right? Maybe you think
forty-nine percent is too much. Maybe you don't want me
for a partner. I'm too vulgar. I'm not a Fifth Avenue person-
ality. All right. I'll tell you what. I'll buy your name."

Winger starts to laugh. "Hey, man," he says, "what is
this? A comedy routine?"

"Come on," Al says, "what's your price?"

Dave says, "What're you talking about? You can't buy my
name."

"Why not?" Al says. "I buy your name, I rent a store, open

the business, and call myself David Winger Home Repair. I get myself a manager, I buy him the safari outfit, he goes around with a clipboard and says he's from David Winger. He looks at a job, gives a price, and subcontracts out the work. The customer pays me because I'm David Winger Home Repair. All I do is advertise and rake in the money."

Dave says, "If you believe that, you can do it without my name."

"No, I can't," Al says. "If I say Albert T. Croppe Home Repair, nobody knows me. Nobody ever heard of me painting, doing electrical, roofing. I can't do that stuff. So I need a name with a reputation. A name like that is gold. All you gotta do is gimme a price."

By that time Al's food is ready. He ordered his usual, which is ham and eggs, scrambled, with french fries, toast, and a Coffee Royale. Genelli brings it out and sets it on the bar. Al sits down and starts to salt his eggs and put ketchup on the fries. Max pours him another Coffee Royale. He looks over at Dave, who's sitting there with just a beer and the Coffee Royale which he hasn't touched, and says to Max, "Give Mr. Winger some eggs. On my tab."

Dave says, "It's okay. Thanks anyway but I already ordered."

Al says, "You already ordered. You know what? I like you. You're an independent bastard. You stand on your own two feet. Nobody's gonna do nothin' for you. Am I right? There's only one problem. You know what the problem is? The problem is that you're not a businessman. Don't get mad. I'm not trying to insult you. I'm speaking frankly because I like you and I wanna give you a break. I'm gonna teach you a few things. Dave, in business a name is gold. It's your most valuable asset. I'll give you the check here and now and we go to a lawyer and sign the papers. Then I own your name. I go into business and I'm David Winger Home Repair. If you want to go into business later, you use some other name."

Dave says, "I'd be pretty stupid to do that."

Al says, "No, you wouldn't. You can make a lot of money that way. It happens all the time. You think every business is owned by the guy who started it? The guy's name is still on it but he sold out long ago. You sell your business and part of the price is the name. That's what accountants call 'Good Will' and, believe me, it goes for a high price because it's valuable. If you sell me your name I go to the bank tomorrow and I'll get fifty thousand dollars to start a business. I can see you don't understand that because you don't understand how business works. That's what I'm tryin' to teach you. In business, the hardest thing to come by is a good reputation and you got that already. If you got that you are a guaranteed money-maker. The banks are looking for guys like you. You're a safe investment. You know, I can't believe I'm talking like this. I'm trying to convince you! I'm drooling here and you can't see it. I don't understand. Listen, I'm so sure that you are a winner that I'll work out any kind of partnership you want. I say we need fifty thousand to start. That's my estimate. You got a better one and I'll be glad to hear it, but I say fifty thousand and I got my twenty-five thousand right here." And he's waving his checkbook. "Just name it and we're in business," he says.

Dave says, "Well, I don't have twenty-five thousand and there's no way I'm ever going to have it so forget it."

"Listen, man," Al says, "if you don't want to do it, that's okay, but don't talk stupid. Don't say you can't get the money because it's not true. All you gotta do is walk into a bank and it's yours. Let's be serious. Let's talk like grown men. Let's understand the finances of this thing. You are a man who is sitting on a fortune. What you are doing is like owning oil leases and deciding just to pay the taxes and not develop them. Suppose you owned a vacant lot and somebody told you there's oil under it but you need fifty thousand dollars to get the oil out. What would you say to him? 'There's no way I'm ever gonna get that money.' Would you say that? Be honest."

Dave says, "If you have oil you can get money."

Al says, "That's just what I'm telling you! You got a reputation and in business that's better than oil. That's gold. A reputation is gold, Dave. Your name is gold around here. I heard where you're talking about. Woodside, Jackson Heights, Sunnyside, Maspeth. You're talking about half a million people, maybe a million people. The banks are looking for somebody like you. You ought to be rich right now. You got so much going for you, you ought to make up some excuse for not being rich. It's embarrassing. You come to the bank with me on Monday morning and in ten minutes you'll walk out of there with twenty-five thousand dollars. I got my twenty-five thousand right here and we're in business. I know people there. I know them all. It's no problem, Dave."

Genelli comes out of the kitchen again and now he's got a plate of manicotti. He puts it down in front of Winger and Winger orders another beer.

Croppe says, "You orderin' beer again? Beer with manicotti? That's Italian food. You don't drink beer with Italian food. You drink red wine. Max, give him a glass of red wine. I'm going to show you the ropes, kid. You start dealing with bankers and businessmen and you got to know about things like wine. When to drink red, when to drink white. This is the kind of thing that goes with money. When you get rich you act rich. Max, red wine! And put everything on my tab."

"I'll have beer," Dave says. "And I got my own money. Take it out of this, Max." He pulls out a wad of tens that he just got from Mrs. Blitnis, peels off two, and lays them on the bar.

Al says, "Max, that's Confederate money. It's no good. Your money's no good here, Dave. Put it away. I'm makin' an investment. You are a gold mine and I'm investing in you. This is my treat. Monday morning you come to the bank with me and I'll show you what I can do for you. And just to show my good faith, I give my pledge right now. Max, gimme a pen!" Max hands him a pen from behind the bar and Al makes out a check. "This is made out to you, David Winger, for twenty-five thousand dollars." He tears it off and tries to hand it to Winger. Winger won't take it. "What's your problem?" Al says. "I don't understand you. Come on. Talk straight. What is the problem?"

Winger says, "Max, do you know this guy?"

Max says, "He's a regular customer."

Al says, "You know, I'm a patient man. Nobody ever calls me a saint but I like to think that I have certain virtues and one of them is patience. In fact I'm more than patient. I am a long-suffering individual. I put up with a lot. But I've never been insulted like this. You've been insulting me since I walked in here and I've got to tell you that I think you're a rude person. All I want to do is hand you this check as an article of faith. All I want to do the whole time I been talking to you is take you in on a serious business deal. I've got Max's word as your reference, and you're not denying what he says, and on just that I'm willing to put up a lot of money. I'm not doing this out of charity. I'm doing it for business. But I am showing good faith. I'm showing faith in you. And what you've been doing the whole time since I came in is making fun of me."

Dave is not the kind of person who makes fun of people. He doesn't insult people. The whole reason he came to New York is to be a nice person—which is something I'll explain later. So this upsets him. He says, "I'm sorry. I never meant to insult you."

Al says, "Then what did you mean?"

Dave says, "I didn't mean anything. But you walk in here and offer to buy my name. I don't know you. I don't know where you come from. I don't know anything about you. The whole thing is very strange."

Al says, "I know it sounds strange to you. To you, working five, six days a week and making just enough money to buy clothes that look like they come from the Salvation Army, that sounds normal. That's why you can't afford a phone. You get your business calls in a bar, for Chrissakes. That's normal to you. That's why any real business deal would sound strange. Look, man, I talk straight. I don't play games." He picks up the two tens Winger laid on the bar. "You worked hard for this money. Am I right?" He tears the bills in half and drops them on the floor. Winger is so surprised he doesn't know what to do. He's just staring at the guy. Al says, "That's what that money is worth. It's nothing, man. I'm talking big money. Max, give him credit for that money. Put it on my tab. Put everything on my tab."

2

~~~~~~

I NEVER PERSONALLY SPOKE TO SID GENERAL. I USED to see him around the neighborhood, but I didn't know who he was until Max told me. He's a big fat guy who wears white suits all the time. I used to see him carrying a white suit in a plastic bag from the French cleaner—which is owned by a Korean. It used to be owned by a Hungarian Jew. Which is how this neighborhood goes. Sid does all his own shopping so I also used to see him with bags of groceries from the supermarket, which he buys to feed his poker game. Max tells me he also does odd jobs. Not odd jobs like cleaning somebody's basement. He's got a big Lincoln Continental and he chauffeurs people around in it for a fee. There are stories around that he's also an enforcer. I'm told he'll do it for whoever pays his price. But I don't know if that's true. What I do know is that his main job is the poker game, which is a twenty-four-hour-a-day, seven-day-a-week operation in his apartment. He sits on a high stool and takes something out of every pot. I've heard it's a dollar, I heard it's five, I heard it's ten, but I don't know which it is.

His face is all bags. People say he never sleeps more than three or four hours a day. Most of the time he sleeps in his car because he's got no furniture in his apartment except stuff for the poker game. He'll drive out to some place like Flushing Meadow Park or a quiet street in Douglaston or College Point and doze off behind the wheel. It's not a healthy way to live if you worry about cholesterol but Sid is more worried about not letting people know ahead of time where he's going to be.

I've been told that it's not unusual for a guy to drop five to ten thousand in one night at that poker game. And this kind of game is cash on the line. You can't get in there without showing three or four thousand. Since Al Croppe is a regular, that tells you something about his financial situation.

Nobody gets into that game unless they have Sid General's personal approval. Now since everybody has Sid's approval, even if the players don't know each other or don't like each other, nobody accuses anybody else of cheating because that would be an insult to Sid. But it just so happens that on the day of the blizzard Al Croppe had the feeling that somebody was cheating. Al had three aces, two of them showing, and a young guy who'd never been there before, who was wearing a white cap which he didn't take off all night and which really bothered Al, was raising him by fifty dollars with only a pair of sevens showing. Al couldn't help thinking that the guy was cheating because otherwise why would he raise him with only a pair of sevens? But he couldn't say anything. Al had those three aces, two showing, and behind that, in the hole, he also had two fives. From the way Al was betting the guy had to know he had more than the two aces. So why was he raising with only those two sevens? Naturally he had a third seven in the hole. Maybe he had a full house. But there is no full house that will beat an aces-high full house, which is what Al had and what this guy should have been figuring Al had. So why wasn't he? He's got that dumb-looking white cap on, which he's been wearing all night when it's so hot in that apartment you could sit in your underwear, and if he wasn't cheating, Al figured, he had to be stupid. So Al is hesitating about whether to raise him or not and at the same time, the pot is getting so big and it's costing him so much money and the guy is raising and raising so much that Al is worried. But he's not going to drop out with an aces-high full house. So he's sitting there and thinking. Should he raise or not? After a while Sid says, "It'll cost you fifty to see him," which is Sid's way of telling him that he's holding up the game. Al does not like that. He's not an amateur, he's not a new guy, and he's not an idiot like Joe—who's sitting behind him on the couch—who loses early and then hangs around. But he still can't figure out what's going on. So he's looking at the guy's sevens.

"You in or out?" Sid says.

"I'm thinkin'," Al says.

"Hey, Al, you ain't got enough brains to think for that long," Joe yells over from the couch.

"He sits back there so he can smell my farts," Al says. He picks up a fifty—which is his last fifty—two twenties, and a ten and puts them in the pot. "I see you and I raise you fifty," he says.

The new guy touches his cap. Maybe it's a good luck charm. He nods his head a couple of times and Al would like to stick his fist in the guy's teeth but naturally he keeps a poker face. The guy picks up a fifty and drops it in the pot.

Al is relieved that all this raising and raising, one on top of the other, is going to end.

"I see you," the guy says, "and I raise you," and he drops in another fifty.

Al would like to spit in the guy's face. What the hell can he have? He's got to have a full house. The guy has a full house and figures Al has three aces and figures he's gonna beat those three aces. Al picks up two twenties and a ten and drops them in the pot. "What've you got?" he says.

"Four of 'em," the guy says and he turns over two more sevens.

"Shit!" Al says and throws down his cards. Now he knows the guy didn't cheat because the guy's an idiot, because only an idiot would stay waiting for a fourth seven when Al al-

ready had two aces showing and was betting so big that he
drove everybody else out.

He gets up from the table and says, "What time is it?" Sid
tells him it's three o'clock.

He says, "A.M. or P.M., for Chrissake?" because the shades
are down and he can't tell.

"How long you think you been here?" Sid says.

Al says, "That's it for me," and he goes to the bathroom.

This apartment looks like somebody just moved out because there's no furniture. There's a bunch of coats on the
floor in the bedroom, a roll of toilet paper in the bathroom,
and the kitchen is full of grocery bags that Sid uses for garbage which Joe takes down to the incinerator every once in a
while. Meanwhile, until he does, the bags are sitting there
full of empty beer cans, pizza crusts, cheese, and whatnot.
It's roach heaven. There's a big coffee pot in there, powdered
cream and sugar, and a stack of paper cups. Then there's
food, like maybe cheese or doughnuts, and beer in the refrigerator.

Al's in the bathroom and he's mad. "Sevens!" he's yelling,
"four sevens!" and they can hear him even while the toilet's
flushing. He comes out and gets his fur coat from the pile on
the floor in the bedroom. Joe's sitting on the couch with his
coat on and he says to him, "Where you goin'?"

Al says, "I'm goin' for breakfast."

"We got stuff here," Sid says.

"Dried-up cheese and beer ain't my idea of breakfast," Al
says. "Eggs is breakfast."

Joe says, "I'll keep you company."

Al says, "No thanks. I gotta make a stop."

You got to realize that the shades are down and nobody has bothered to look outside so they don't know it's snowing.

Joe says, "I ain't doin' nothin'. I got all day. I'll wait for you."

"You can't come," Al says. "I'm stopping at the Yoga Institute. I'm doing meditation for the rest of the afternoon."

"Come on, Al," Joe says. "Is he kidding about that yogi stuff or what?" But the guys are into another hand and they don't hear him.

Al goes out and gets the elevator. He went to the poker game after midnight and there was no sign of snow. The forecast didn't mention snow. They said it was going to snow south of here, in Washington and Baltimore, maybe Philly, but not here. Maybe a few flurries or something like that. Now he gets out of the elevator and the first thing he sees through the glass door in the lobby is the blizzard. It's a foot deep and blowing like crazy. This amazes him. He never suspected it for a minute the whole time he was in there. This is why I consider poker players stupid. They go in there, pull down the shades, stay twelve, twenty-four hours, and don't know what's going on outside. They don't know if it's day or night. The world could come to an end and if it didn't make any noise they wouldn't know about it.

Al goes to the Green Leaf Tavern and that's where he meets Winger.

3

DAVE WINGER DID NOT START OUT IN LIFE TO BE A plumber or a house painter. And I can tell you that he won't end up that way either. I used to sit and drink beer with Dave Winger in the Green Leaf Tavern and we had some long talks. He comes from a college-educated family in Ohio which makes good money and is not used to doing the kind of work Dave is doing here. I believe this was a case of a kid rebelling against his family. His father teaches college. His brother is a lawyer and his sister is married to some big executive. Dave tells me he gets his know-how about electricity and working with his hands from a grandfather who made a fortune as an inventor for things they use on farms. He also had an uncle who was an artist. So you can see that although he's working with his hands, he's not doing it because he has to. He's doing it for an idea. A theory. He says to me he wants to know what life is all about. He says that sitting in an office and making money isn't his idea of life. I said to him, "What, in your opinion, is your idea of life?" He says, "I'm not sure but right now I think the best a person can do is if other people say, 'My life is better because of him.'"

Well that's very nice and I have no objection to it. But if you think about it, you'll see that it's the kind of thing only rich people can do—people who have the time and money to do what they want. To me that's like playing. As far as the rest of us are concerned, we don't have time to find out what life is all about because we have to make a living. In fact, if I did find out what life is all about it wouldn't make any difference to me because I'd still have to make a living. So as far as I'm concerned, even though he lives here, works just as hard as anybody else, and drinks beer with me in the Green Leaf, Dave Winger is still living a different kind of life and is a different kind of person.

For instance, one night we're sitting and talking and I asked him why he quit college. He says to me that college wasn't teaching him anything real. He wanted to get out in the real world, meet real people and see real life. Now we're sitting in the Green Leaf and talking. This is what he chose to do. So what does that mean? I've got to assume that sitting here and talking is what he means by real life and I'm the real people he's talking about. I don't know how to take that. Is it a compliment or an insult or what? And what is real life? If sitting and talking in a bar is real life then everything must be real life. So what is he talking about?

I resented that kind of talk. I don't have a college education to throw away for deep ideas and I don't do saintly work because I have to support a family. I work twelve-hour shifts five days a week and I don't have the time or strength for anything else. But let's put that aside. Let's talk about him. I have to admit that he was not a hypocrite. At least he tried not to be a hypocrite. He came out here, got a cheap place to live, and took odd jobs. Mostly he worked for old people and he didn't charge them much. So he had what you might call a special clientele because this area has a lot of old people and they passed his name around from one to the next. Most of them don't have a lot of money. And I can tell you they're not big tippers either. When they have a problem with their houses they let it go because it's too expensive to fix. But now here comes Dave Winger and he works cheap and does a beautiful job. Once word of that got around the man had more business than he could handle. Then he had a reputation and he could have worked anywhere and charged anything. But he didn't. I give him credit. He kept working for the same kind of people as before and not charging much. But don't get the wrong impression. These are not all poor people. They're not starving. They don't have it easy and they live close to the vest but some of them own houses. In fact, I wouldn't be surprised if some of them had plenty of money socked away. I said that to Dave but he didn't care. That kind of stuff didn't bother him because he liked working for these people. He liked the people, all of them—crackpots, cheapskates, senile, the whole works. And once the people got to know him, when he spent a few days working in their houses, they liked him. They loved him. You have to see some of these old people. I get them in my cab. They're slow, maybe they got arthritis, maybe they're hard of hearing or they don't see too well, and everybody takes advantage of them. But not Winger. And they appreciate that. They love him. They think he's a saint.

Let me tell you how he operates. I once went with him to give an estimate. The way that happened has to do with the way Queens is laid out. This area, central Queens—I'm talking about Elmhurst, Maspeth, Jackson Heights, Woodside, Astoria—in this whole area nothing is straight except the main avenues like Queens Boulevard, Northern Boulevard, and Broadway. Everything else is broken up. You're on a street and all of a sudden it ends. Then it picks up again someplace else which you can't find. The buses aren't going to go on that kind of street. They stick to the main routes. The subways go to Manhattan so they're no help. The only way to get around here is to walk or take a cab or a car service like the one I work for. That is expensive for the average person. With the tip you can't get away for less than five dollars on the cheapest ride. When Winger goes to price a job he'll walk or take a bus but sometimes he just can't and he winds up in a cab. One day, by coincidence, I got the call. I took him to a place on a side street off Calamus Avenue and he says to me, "Do you want to come in?" I radioed in that I was getting off the seat, which you're allowed to do for a few minutes as long as you're in the area, and I went with him.

He rings the bell and through the window we can see his customer coming. She's holding on to one of these aluminum walkers and moving so slow that it takes forever. She's got a bottle of nitro pills in her hand like she's expecting a heart attack any minute. To open the door she has to open two locks and two chains and push back a bolt. It took her so long and was so hard that I didn't think she could do it. But she managed and she lets us into the living room. The place is full of old pictures. Nothing's been moved since her husband died, which was probably back when Eisenhower was president. It smells like his coffin is still in the dining room. She says to Winger she wants a paint job, no extras. He looks around and gives her a price on the low side because he feels sorry for her. She heard he's cheap so she's expecting he'll give her a price that would have been cheap twenty years ago and she thinks this price is high so she's not happy. But she figures she's not going to do better and he comes highly recommended so she says okay. After we leave I said to him, "You're not going to make a living with prices that low."

A couple of days later he comes to work. He looks around and decides he can't paint yet. He's got to take off the old moldings and buy new ones because the old ones had so many coats of paint on them that they'll chip in a few weeks if he paints over them and he can't work that way. Then he looks at the electric outlets and decides they're so old they might cause a fire and he can't let an old lady live in that condition. So he replaces them. Then he spackles, sands, and caulks, even though it wasn't part of the deal. Then he washes the walls so he doesn't have to paint over dirt and grease. Finally he paints. All those extras make the job last a day, maybe two days longer and cost him more in materials than he figured on but he says to himself that he can't charge her for any of it because he already gave her the price.

Now this is all very nice and these people really are better off because of him. So he has his wish. But let's face it. He couldn't do this if he really had to make a living. That is why, from the very beginning, from the first time he told me his story, I always believed that one day Winger would either go back home or change the way he does business.

But that's all right. I don't hold that against him. I look at it this way. I hope that when I get old there's another kid like him around, trying to do good, who'll fix up my place for me.

4

ON THE DAY OF THE BLIZZARD WINGER WAS WORK-
ing at the Blitnises' apartment on Ketchem
Street. The Blitnises loved him. Mrs. Blitnis
was always running down to the bakery,
buying cake and putting it on the kitchen
table for him. She kept a pot of coffee hot
and she was always telling him, "Mr.
Winger, take a break. You work too hard."
Of course she's not paying him by the hour
so if the job takes longer it costs him money,
not her. But he enjoys it and she means
well. They sit in the kitchen and talk and
the Blitnises can't get enough of him. These
are lonely people. Nobody visits them. The

children are in California or Texas or maybe they're only in
Manhattan but I know they're never on Ketchem Street. So
having Winger there is big stuff and they don't want to miss
a second. Mr. Blitnis is a guy who reads all day, he's got
glasses as thick as window panes, but as soon as Winger
comes into the kitchen for a break he shuts his book and
comes in to talk. He's a philosopher. Mrs. Blitnis said to me,
"If he wasn't such a philosopher we'd have enough money
to retire in Florida. We had a grocery store for thirty-seven
years. I did all the work and he read books. If he sold philosophy and made some money I'd say, 'All right,' but he never
sold any philosophy. All he did was read."

Mr. Blitnis doesn't pay attention to this. All he's interested in is books and he's always talking about what he's
reading. He tells Winger there was a Greek philosopher who
said you shouldn't eat beans. Another philosopher, Aristotle, spoke from cards. I don't know what that means but I
suppose this kind of information is educational.

Mrs. Blitnis serves Winger on her good dishes, like he's a
guest of honor. Winger tells her not to because he has paint
on his hands. She says, "Don't worry. They're old. I bought
this set in Washington, D.C., on my honeymoon when
Franklin Delano Roosevelt was president." And they look it.
But it was a nice thing for her to do.

When he's halfway through the job and they can see how
nice it's going to be, Mrs. Blitnis sits him down and says to
him, "Mr. Winger, I want to tell you something. You're a
nice man. You talk nice and you're respectful. You don't
cheat people. You do good work and you're conscientious of
the senior citizen."

He could do worse than go through life with that to re-member. Sometimes a memory like that makes you more willing to be decent in later years. Of course there's also the people who do one decent thing in life and from then on figure they got a license to be a bastard.

The Friday of the blizzard Winger got an early start be-cause he knew he was going to finish the job that day and he wanted to finish early. When he walked to Ketchem Street the snow was just starting. He got to work, skipped lunch, and around one or two o'clock he's finished. He packs up his tools in a big canvas bag which he made himself and he's ready to leave. Mrs. Blitnis is all choked up. She can't believe she's never going to see him again. Mr. Blitnis isn't reading. He's hanging around like he wants to say something but doesn't know what. Mrs. Blitnis says, "Come up and visit us. Take a look at your work. You should have pride and enjoy it." He says he'll try. She goes to the bedroom and gets his money out of a drawer. This is a straight cash business. Nothing written down. She went to the bank when it opened that morning and got the money, all in tens.

She says, "Here's your money, Mr. Winger. You earned it. You did a beautiful job and I'm well satisfied. Let me count it over so I'm sure I'm not cheating you." And she starts to put the bills down one at a time on the kitchen table. "Ten, twenty, thirty, forty, fifty . . . You'll get some business on account of me," she says. "I already told some people about you."

He says, "Thank you."

She says, "It's the least I can do. I wish I had a mansion for you to paint. Now where was I? Maybe I better start over."

And she picks up the bills and starts over. "Ten, twenty, thirty, forty, fifty, sixty, seventy . . . The only thing is you should get a phone. It makes a bad impression to leave a message at a bar. Some people will think you're a drinker or something like that. I know it's not true but people get the wrong idea."

He says, "You're right. I should."

She says, "Where did I leave off?"

He says, "Seventy."

She says, "Are you sure?" She looks at the tens on the table and she's trying to see if it looks like seven but she can't tell. She wants to show him that she takes his word but she can't do it. So she fiddles around and stalls and finally she picks up the money and starts over. "Ten, twenty, thirty, forty, fifty . . ." and this time she gets it all counted. But she still doesn't hand it to him. She says, "You know, Mr. Winger, I'm so pleased with this job that I'm going to give you a tip."

He says, "That's very nice of you, Mrs. Blitnis, but you don't have to."

She says, "Melody Watson in the first race Tuesday. I got inside information." Then she gives him the money.

Winger never played the tip. Can you believe that? I'm not a gambler but the lady said she had inside information. For five dollars you take a chance.

He puts the wad of tens in his pocket and goes out. And he's surprised by the snow too. By then it's over his ankles and it's coming down in this terrific wind. He doesn't know what to do. In that blizzard it could take an hour to walk to the Green Leaf. And when he gets there the place could be closed. He could freeze to death in that time. But if he doesn't go to the Green Leaf he'll just go back to his room and hole up there with all that money in his pocket and eat tuna fish, which he doesn't want to do. It's a longer walk to his room than it is to the Green Leaf and in that weather there's going to be no buses, cabs, or anything. He could go someplace else, there's a million places, but that doesn't occur to him. He starts walking to Broadway. By the way, whenever I mention Broadway here I'm talking about Broadway in Queens, not the famous one in Manhattan. This is a very different street. I don't even know why they call it Broadway. He goes to Broadway, past Elmhurst Hospital, and keeps heading toward Roosevelt. It's not a long walk but in the snow he can't even make out the El. After a couple of blocks he's got ice on the bottoms of his pants, his shoes and socks are soaked through, and his feet are frozen. His face feels like ice and he's covered with snow.

Most of the stores are closed. Nobody's doing business. The storekeepers who stayed open are looking out their windows with their hands behind their backs. He passes a shoe store which is still open and he goes in. He buys shoes and socks and puts his old wet stuff in the canvas bag which is frozen stiff by now. Then he asks for a pair of rubbers.

I happen to know this salesman. I bought shoes there myself. He's an obnoxious person. He says to Winger, "Rubbers won't do you any good out there. The weather report is for twelve to fourteen inches. You need boots on a day like this."

Winger says, "It must be that high now. I didn't even know it was supposed to snow."

The guy says, "Last night I heard three different weather forecasts and not one of 'em said it would snow. Can you believe that? These guys make half a million dollars a year. They have fan clubs. And they can't forecast the weather. They don't know anything about the weather. They can't forecast the weather. All they do is read it off a card. You or I could do the same thing. But they get away with it. You know why? Because the public is stupid. You deal with the public every day like I do and you'll see what I mean. Listen, you don't want rubbers. I got something for you in boots. A waterproof boot that will last you ten years."

He brings out an old box which looks like it's been in the basement and pulls out a pair of orange rubber boots with a blue line around the tops and says, "I can give you a good price on these."

Winger takes a look and says, "I don't think so." He can't say no straight out, not to a guy like this, a guy who comes in to work on the worst day of the year and must be desperate for a sale. But these boots are ugly.

The guy says, "Try 'em on. In snow like this it's the only thing that'll keep you dry. They're not the fashion but what do you care what the fairies in Manhattan are wearing? You want a boot that'll keep you dry."

Winger doesn't want these boots but ten minutes later he comes into the Green Leaf Tavern and he's wearing them.

5

SO IN ALL THAT SNOW HE GOES TO THE GREEN LEAF
and that's where he meets Croppe. Croppe
gives him the song and dance about David
Winger Home Repair and to tell you the
truth I have no idea if he's serious or not.
Maybe Croppe himself doesn't know. The
man talks. It's like he puts out a hundred
lines with bait on them and if he catches
something, okay, if not, that's okay too.
Maybe if Dave took him up at that moment,
when he wrote the check, everything would
have come out different. It's one of those
things nobody'll ever know.

Dave is sitting there eating his manicotti,

drinking beer, not touching the red wine or the Coffee Royale, and he's looking at the slip of paper which Max gave him. He's got three hundred fifty dollars in his pocket from Mrs. Blitnis. When I first met him, if he had cash like that in his pocket he wouldn't bother with another big job. He'd give himself a couple of days off. But this time he goes out, right in the middle of the blizzard, someplace Croppe can't hear him, and makes the call. I think he was getting a little tired of not having money so he was ready to go for two big jobs in a row. So he leaves the bar and he has no more to say to Croppe and Croppe has no more to say to him.

He calls the number on the slip and the lady is surprised to hear from him in the middle of a blizzard. But she says to come over the next day, which is Saturday, and give her an estimate. He goes over there, gives the estimate, she says okay and tells him to start Monday. It's a big job which will take him a week. And it's in Maspeth which would be two or three buses for him. That is a lot of money so Monday morning he decides to walk. Most of the sidewalks are shoveled by then but it's bitter cold. There's no straight route from his place to hers. He's got to get over dead ends and under the railroad. In places like that the snow is piled high. When he finally gets there he's wet and he feels like he already put in a day's work. And right from the start the lady is nasty. She happens to be a very ugly person also. There's no coffee and cake on this job.

He's supposed to paint the whole downstairs—a kitchen, bathroom, dining room, living room, plus a foyer or vestibule, a little space by the front door for hanging up coats.

First off, he looks around to see how he's going to go about the job. She's right there with him, watching like a hawk, like he's going to steal something. He says to her, "I think I'll start in the living room."

She says, "Why the living room? Start in the kitchen."

If he said he was going to start in the kitchen she'd say, "Start in the living room." He should have said to her, "Look, lady, I do it my way or else get yourself a different painter." But Winger is not like that. He knows he could walk out and get a different job for the same money but he feels sorry for her—an ugly old lady who lives alone in a filthy place. That's how he is with these people. Like he owes them something. So he explains to her why he wants to start in the living room and finally she says okay. That doesn't mean she's happy. She's the type of person who's never going to be happy. But he figures that when he gets a few rooms done and she sees how the place looks she'll feel better and she'll be nicer. When he told me the story I said to him if that's all it took to make people nice they wouldn't put criminals in jails, they'd put them in fancy apartments. He says to me that in Scandinavia they do. I don't know about Scandinavia and I don't know if that's true so I dropped the subject.

He starts out by washing her living room walls. The walls are so filthy that just washing them gets them so much cleaner that she's already thinking they don't need a paint job. She has a devious mind so naturally she figures everybody else is just as devious and she figures that if the walls don't need a paint job he's not going to paint them. He's going to fake it. He'll tell her the water is paint, or something like that. So she starts another argument. It's so ridiculous that he doesn't know what she's talking about. Finally he says to her, "Mrs. Dellawood, if you want me to paint over the grease and dirt, I'll do that. I usually wash it off but if it bothers you, I'll just paint right over it."

She backs off but she keeps watching him like a hawk to make sure he uses paint after he washes.

By late in the afternoon he's ready to paint. Mrs. Dellawood is in the kitchen. She's got her TV on, she's watching quiz shows and drinking coffee. Naturally she doesn't offer him any. He's up on the ladder and he starts the ceiling. He's working away up there when all of a sudden the doorbell rings. She goes to the foyer and opens the door. Winger hears a girl's voice, which surprises him. He figured this nasty old lady wouldn't know anybody. The girl and the old lady start to make a big fuss over each other out there and he hears the young one calling Mrs. Dellawood "Aunt Dell." They come into the living room and Winger can't believe his eyes. This is a beautiful girl. She's about Winger's age, very sexy and dressed very nice. He can't figure how an ugly old lady like Mrs. Dellawood gets to have a beautiful niece like this. The girl could be an actress. He says, "Hello," and she answers polite enough but she doesn't really pay attention to him. He can't take his eyes off her. He's painting but he keeps trying to look at her. But she doesn't know he's there. It's like he's part of the ladder. The two of them, the aunt and the niece, who is named Kathy, go into the kitchen and have coffee and talk. He's up on the ladder painting but he's listening to them. He's dying for her to come out and talk to him. He figures she's got to come out sooner or later. But she doesn't. She sits in the kitchen with Aunt Dell talking about her job. He's taking in every word. She's a commercial artist in an advertising agency. She's telling stories about ad campaigns and conferences, and everything is for big money. Aunt Dell is going tsk, tsk over everything the girl says.

He finishes for the day and they're still in the kitchen. He cleans up, packs his stuff, and goes in to talk to her. But he can't get a conversation going because she's not interested. He hangs out in the doorway trying to get her to pay attention to him but she won't.

The next day he can't wait to see if the girl comes back. Sure enough, around four o'clock the doorbell rings and there she is again. Now I believe that what's happening here—the reason for these visits—is that the old lady has money. Why else would this girl run out there every day? What she's doing is trying to make sure she's in the will. Naturally Winger doesn't think of that. He takes a look at this girl and he can't think straight.

She's a little friendlier this time because she saw him before but she's still not interested. She looks at what he's done and then goes into the kitchen with Aunt Dell and they sit there and talk again. This time the conversation is about promotions. The girl got a raise three months ago and now she wants another one. She's talking about other people's salaries and it's all big numbers. This one is getting a six-figure salary and that one got a twenty-five-thousand-dollar raise last month. They're telling her she's got to wait at least six months before they'll consider giving her another raise but she's on the fast track and she doesn't want to be slowed down so she's thinking of changing jobs.

Winger is doing his usual beautiful work. The girl even says to her aunt, "It's beautiful." Winger is standing right there but she doesn't say it to him. It's like she doesn't see him. Every day that week she comes to visit Aunt Dell. She's always discussing promotions, raises, big money, and Winger is taking in every word. This is a beautiful girl and it's driving him nuts. Even when he's not on the job he's thinking about her. He can't imagine why she won't look at him. Every day he's thinking of what he can say to her to get her attention but nothing works.

Now you would think, if he's not interested in money, that the way she talks about money would turn him off. But it doesn't. Which to me is suspicious. But I have to admit there are also other things going on here. First of all, this is a very beautiful girl. Second of all, he's a young guy, in his twenties, and he's lonely. He's got no money and he's not traveling in the kind of circles he's used to so he's not meeting the more educated type of girl he's used to. I suspect that when it comes to sex and female companionship, he's probably getting desperate. When he sees this girl he's so anxious he forgets the ideals he likes to tell me about and just goes after her. His problem is that he's so anxious that he doesn't understand why she's not interested in him.

Finally it's his last day on the job. Mrs. Dellawood is as happy as she's ever going to be. Her place never looked so good. She knows he's not going to cheat her. She's probably thinking of how to cheat him. But all he's thinking about is the girl and for this last day, he's got a plan. He's going to tell her about his uncle who was an artist. Since the girl is a commercial artist he figures she'll be interested enough to get a conversation going.

He's already putting on the last touches when she comes in. She comes over to look at what he's doing and he says to her—but cool, like he hasn't been thinking about this all last night and all day today—"Hi. I couldn't help overhearing what you've been telling your aunt. I heard you say you're an artist. My uncle was an artist. He painted landscapes."

She says, "That's nice."

He says, "Out in Ohio. He had exhibitions at some of the colleges. He sold a lot of paintings." She doesn't say anything to that. He says, "This room is finished. The whole job is done. I guess that's it." He's letting her know that she's got to speak up if she wants to get anywhere with him. It's now or never. But the girl doesn't even know what he's talking about. He doesn't understand that because he wants this girl so bad. He starts talking about art and painting again, like that's really going to get her interested, but in the middle of what he's saying she walks away and starts talking to Aunt Dell. That's when it finally dawns on him. For some reason, all of a sudden, he realizes how he must look to her. When she looks at him she sees a house painter, a poor guy in old clothes. When he talked to me, he could imagine that that meant he was a real person. But this girl is not interested in that kind of real person. She's interested in six-figure salaries. So when Winger finally sees this he doesn't say another word. He doesn't look at her again. He picks up his tools and all he wants to do is get out of there.

Meanwhile, the two of them, the old lady and the niece, are walking around looking at the job. They're looking for defects. They don't find any so the old lady comes out and gives him his money in an envelope. It's all cash, no receipt, no record, but he doesn't count it. He just shoves it in his pocket. He's so disgusted he doesn't care. And this is serious because if she didn't put in the full amount, once he walks out the door there's nothing he can do about it.

He's ready to go but all of a sudden the niece, Kathy, calls her aunt. She found a defect. The old lady calls him back and tells him to fix it. He doesn't argue. He unpacks his tools and takes care of it. Meanwhile they keep walking around, looking for more defects. He finishes and he's ready to go again. The girl is in the room watching him. All of a sudden, without thinking about anything, he says to her, "Next week I'm opening my own business."

She doesn't say anything. She's still looking for defects. But then, like she's being polite, she says, "What kind of business?"

He says, "I'm calling it David Winger Home Repair. I won't do this work myself any more. I'm hiring other people to do it."

She nods but she doesn't say anything.

He says, "Your aunt is lucky. After this my prices will go up. This is just kind of a training program I'm giving myself. I don't want to be in a position where I send people out to do work that I haven't done myself."

She looks at him. She says, "Really? That's interesting."

He says, "You'll probably be seeing my ads."

She says, "Who's doing them?"

He says, "I haven't decided yet. I've been concentrating on this part first—getting the experience. You can't run a business unless you've done the work yourself."

She says, "You mean you do all this painting and housework just for experience?"

He says, "Yes, of course. Otherwise I wouldn't do it."

She says, "You mean you don't have to do it?"

He says, "No, I'm just trying to learn the business."

She says, "But how do you make a living? Do you make enough from this kind of work?"

He says, "Oh, no. Not if you're doing just one job like this. There's no money in it this way."

She says, "Then how do you make a living?"

He says, "I have money."

She says, "Really? Then I have to give you credit—I mean to go out and do this kind of work. But you're very smart to do it. It's the only way to learn a business. But it takes a lot of nerve, I mean to go out as a house painter when you don't have to. But I hope you realize how much money it takes to start a business. If you're going to do it on a big scale."

He says, "Oh, sure. If I don't do it on a big scale it's not worth it. I've got the money. All I needed was the experience."

She says, "You'll need advertising, bookkeeping, payroll help, legal advice. It can cost thousands. Are you sure you can raise that much money?"

He says, "It's no problem. I have the money."

She says, "Do you have backers?"

He says, "No. I'm using my own money."

She says, "That's wonderful. And you certainly have the

right attitude. You're out there learning the nitty-gritty. Meeting the public. A lot of businesses fail because people don't know who they're selling to. It's very exciting to start something new. All on your own. How much do you think it will cost to start up?"

He says, "I figure I'll have to put in between fifty and a hundred thousand dollars before I turn a profit."

She says, "Have you thought of what will happen if you don't succeed? That's a lot of money. I'm sure you'll succeed, but anything can happen. Even if it's not your own fault. That's a lot of money. What will you do if you lose it?"

He says, "I'll try something else. Money is no problem. I'm not worried about that."

She pulls up a chair, sits down, and offers him a cup of coffee. She's got more questions. He doesn't tell her he lives in a furnished room in Jackson Heights and that he dropped out of college to meet real people. They talk about business. They talk about banks. They talk about advertising. He talks about growing up in a small college town in Ohio. He tells stories about his uncle, the black sheep of the family, and she laughs. He mentions that his brother's a lawyer and his father's a college professor. She can't get over him. She can't get over how he has the guts to go out on his own and work with his hands. What she doesn't say but what she can't get over most of all is that money is no problem to him.

He walks out of there about an hour later and he's got her name and phone number on a piece of paper that smells from perfume.

SATURDAY AFTERNOON, A WEEK AFTER THE BLIZ-
zard, I'm sitting in the Green Leaf talking to
Max. Max works six days, 2 P.M. to 10 P.M. I
would not work that schedule for anything.
That's the worst shift I ever heard of. But
that's what he does and I understand it's his
choice.

I'm usually in the Green Leaf on Saturday
afternoon because I don't work Saturdays.
Saturday is not a good day to drive a cab.
What you get on Saturday is women going
to the hairdresser or taking their kids shopping, which puts the kids and the women in
a bad mood and isn't worth the trouble.

They don't tip good either. And you get long periods of time when there're no customers at all. So Saturday is my free day. I go out with my wife on Saturday night but the afternoon is mine. I don't do much. Maybe I go for a walk or see a movie at matinee prices or I go to the Green Leaf—but it's my time. Brenda never asks me what I do Saturday afternoon and I never tell her. I make it a point not to tell her. Not that I do anything I need to keep secret but if some day I do something she doesn't have to know about, it's better that I've been keeping things to myself all along than if I have to start suddenly.

While I'm talking to Max, Dave Winger comes in. He's flush with money because he finished the Dellawood job and he's still got money left from Mrs. Blitnis. Now he's dealing in twenties instead of tens. He lays a twenty on the bar and orders a beer. Max gives him a couple of slips of paper with his calls. He draws the beer and pushes back the twenty and says, "You're covered."

Dave says, "What are you talking about?"

Max says, "It's on Al Croppe's tab. He owes you twenty."

Dave says, "Did he tell you to do that?"

Max says, "You heard him."

Dave says, "I didn't believe him."

Max says, "He said it so he meant it."

Dave says, "Has he been in today?"

Max says, "I didn't notice." Of course that doesn't mean anything. Max is a nice guy but he is not going to give out information about Al Croppe. If anything, he'll give information to Al Croppe. Al is a big tipper. That buys him a lot of eyes and ears and some very closed mouths. So if you're dealing with Al Croppe you got to be careful who you talk to and what you say.

Dave says, "You think he'll be in?"

Max says, "I can't predict Al Croppe."

Dave says, "I'd like to talk to him."

Now I'm listening to this and I'm thinking it's very strange. First of all, I didn't even know Dave knew Al Croppe. At that point nobody told me yet that they had that long conversation on the day of the blizzard. So I'd like to know why he's looking for Al Croppe. He should stay away from people like Al Croppe. And he should know that without me telling him.

But he says, "If you see him, would you tell him I was looking for him?"

Max says, "Sure."

A customer down at the other end of the bar calls for a drink so Max goes down there. As soon as he goes away I say to Dave, "Why are you looking for Al Croppe?" But Dave doesn't want to talk. He's looking in his beer. He shrugs. This surprises me. I say, "I wouldn't mess with a guy like that."

He says, "Why not?"

Now that is a stupid question. Dave Winger is supposed to be smart. He's got high ideals. He's got a college education—at least part of one. He knows about jails in Scandinavia. He talks philosophy with Mr. Blitnis. But here he is asking for a con man who does nothing all day, twenty-four hours a day, three hundred sixty-five days a year, except go

around conning people out of their money. So I say to him—
and, believe me, it's so obvious I feel foolish saying it—I say,
"If you know anything about Al Croppe you should know
that Al Croppe is not a guy for you to mess with." But he
doesn't want to talk about it. And that annoyed me. I'm only
a cabdriver so I'm not supposed to be smart. But if he's such
a big thinker how come I have to teach him not to piss in the
sink? I get up and say, "Brenda is expecting me to take her to
the movies. I gotta go." And I'm mad.

A couple of days go by and late one night Dave is up in his
room and he hears the doorbell. There's a separate doorbell
in that house for each of the roomers. There're three of
them, and they're all sharing one bathroom. Very high class.
This is the first time anybody rung his bell so he's not sure
what it is. At first he thinks it's a fire. He goes downstairs
and opens the door and it's Al Croppe.

"I'm just passing your street," Al says, "so I rang your bell.
I only got a minute. I hear you want to talk to me."

Dave says, "I wanted to talk about the business deal you
mentioned."

Al says, "It's eleven o'clock at night. I can't talk business
now." And he's looking at his watch.

Dave says, "When can we talk?"

Al says, "What's it about?"

Dave says, "I'm interested in what you said. You remember? In the Green Leaf."

Al's making faces like he's in a big hurry and he says, "I'll
tell you what. I'm keeping some people waiting but you're a

good kid so I'm going to give you a few minutes. What's your proposition?"

Winger brings him up to his room, which is furnished with landlord-type furniture. An old tan linoleum with blue flowers on the floor. They sit down and Winger says to him, "I decided I'd like to hear about that business proposition—what we were talking about in the Green Leaf."

Croppe says, "Oh, yeah? What made you decide that?"

Dave says, "I thought it over."

Croppe says, "You thought it over? That's a problem. You took too long. That was a one-day special."

Winger can't tell if the guy is serious or not. So he's already uncomfortable. Maybe he's also sorry he started this. His brain got a little cloudy because of the girl but once he talks to Croppe, gets him in his room and sees him up close like that, reality sets in and he cools off. But Croppe doesn't get up to go. He sits there. If the offer is closed, why is he sitting there? The trouble is that Dave doesn't understand a guy like Croppe. What Croppe is doing is waiting to hear what Dave really wants. He figures Dave has a deal to offer him. Otherwise why would he want to see him? But Dave is not in Croppe's league. So nothing happens. Finally Croppe says, "If you got an idea, lay it out for me."

Dave says, "I'm just talking about what you said that day in the Green Leaf."

Croppe says, "Is that all?"

Dave says, "That's what I said."

Croppe says, "All right, let me tell you what the situation

is. You're talking about that day we had a blizzard. Am I right? The Green Leaf was warm and the two of us were trapped in there. So I made you an offer. I made a very generous offer. It was too generous. I'm not going to make an offer like that again. I'm a serious businessman. Now I don't have a lot of time so don't play games. If you got a proposition, I'll listen. I'm always ready to hear a proposition."

Dave says, "I was just thinking of what you said at the Green Leaf. I wanted to do what you said. You said I would put up the reputation and the know-how and you'd put up the money."

Croppe says, "You think that's a reasonable thing for me to do?"

Dave says, "It was your suggestion."

Croppe says, "And how much do you think your reputation and know-how are worth?"

Dave says, "I don't know. What do you think?"

Croppe says, "I don't think they're worth shit."

Al himself told him that his reputation was gold. Now Al turns around and tells him the opposite. So Dave is shocked. He's insulted. Maybe he's embarrassed. He sits there like his head was cut off.

Al says, "How many people around here know you?"

Dave says, "I don't know."

Al says, "I never heard of you. There are maybe a thousand, maybe ten thousand handymen around here. How are you different?"

Dave is quiet.

"You see what I'm saying?" Al says. "Let's be realistic.

You're putting up shit and you want me to put up fifty thousand dollars."

"I don't think it would take that much," Dave says.

Al says, "You don't know what you're talking about. You ask me for money but you don't have enough experience to know how much it costs to get a business started. You need fifty thousand dollars and not a penny less. But I'll tell you what I'll do. I'll put up half. If you can raise twenty-five thousand I'll put in the other twenty-five thousand. And I'm only doing it for one reason. I like your nerve. That's what you got going for you. There's not two guys in a million who'd have the nerve to call me in here and do what you just did. You were nasty to me that day. You were rude. Like my money wasn't real. And now you ask me for fifty thousand dollars. And you got nothing to offer in return. That takes a lot of nerve. But I give you credit because nerve is what you need in business. So I'm going to take a chance on you. You come up with twenty-five thousand and I'll put in twenty-five thousand." And he's looking at his watch like he's in a hurry.

Dave says, "Look, I'll tell you the truth. The whole point of my asking you was that I can't raise that kind of money. If I could I wouldn't need a partner."

Al looks at him like he's suspicious and says, "So whatever I say, it keeps coming back to the same thing. You want me to put up all the money. Do I have it right?"

Dave is embarrassed but he nods and says, "I guess so."

Al gives him a disgusted look. This makes Dave uncomfortable and he starts to talk, which is always a mistake, and he's stuttering and sputtering and he says, "Well, if you don't like it . . . it was just an idea . . . you mentioned it in the Green Leaf . . . ," and this, that, and the other.

Al puts up his hand. He says, "I don't like being played for a sucker."

Dave says, "I wasn't doing that."

Al says, "I'll tell you what I'm going to do. I think you are a sharp operator. But I am too. You're smart but you're not smarter than me. We're equals. The two of us. Okay? So I am going to go partners with you. Fifty-fifty. But I don't go into a partnership in which I take all the risks. You want to be in business, then you got to put up half. I want you to put up twenty-five thousand and I'm going to show you how to get it. We will go to the bank together tomorrow morning and you will take out a loan which they will give you on my say-so. My recommendation is all you need. How is that for a proposition?"

Now Dave hesitates. He did not expect to have to put himself on the line with a bank for that much money. I don't know what he expected. The truth is, he didn't know either because he wasn't thinking about it. He was thinking about the girl. He didn't expect things to happen so fast. Maybe, in the back of his mind, he figured they'd negotiate back and forth for a while and somehow that would help him get the girl into bed. Who knows what he thought? But if he was really smart he'd have backed out right then and there—as soon as Croppe made the offer. It would have been embarrassing and it would have made Croppe very mad but it would have saved him. But it's a funny thing about people.

They're more ready to go sign up with a bank for twenty-five thousand dollars and get into a lot of trouble than they are to let themselves be embarrassed in front of a con man.

So he thinks it over and says, "Sure. I'm ready for that. I'd rather have my money in it anyway. I just didn't think a bank would give me that kind of loan."

Croppe says, "Don't worry about the bank. If you're with me you can get any kind of a loan you want. But you got to understand some basics. With banks, looks is everything. You can't walk into a bank the way you dress. You got to look like a businessman. The first thing you need is a suit. Let me see your best suit."

Dave says, "I don't own a suit."

Al says, "Then we'll get you a suit."

Dave says, "I don't have money for a suit."

Al says, "When you're with me you don't need money. I'll take care of the money. Let's go."

Dave says, "It's after eleven. Nothing's open now."

Al says, "The people I deal with are open all night."

THEY GO DOWN TO A BAR ON NORTHERN BOULE-
vard and call a cab. By then it must be 11:30
and Winger keeps saying he can't believe a
clothing store will be open that late at night.
Croppe says, "Don't worry about it." The
cab takes them up Ditmars Boulevard in
Astoria to one of the streets in the Forties
near Steinway. By the time they get there
it's midnight. Winger is expecting a big
store all lit up with neon lights. He figures
it's got to be a flashy place if it's open all
night. But this is a dark street and it's dead
quiet. They get out in front of a big white
house with a screen porch next to a church.

Winger looks around and sees nothing. Al starts walking up the path to this big white house. The place is abandoned. The screens are still up in the middle of the winter. Nobody shoveled the walk and there're footprints all over the snow, like a lot of people were walking around in the yard. Al starts heading toward the house and his feet are going *crunch, crunch* in the snow. Dave yells, "Where're you going?" Al goes around the side of the house. Dave runs after him. It's pitch black in the back but he sees some steps going down to a basement door. Al is already down there. Dave is afraid of slipping on the ice but he goes down after him. Al rings a bell. Dave says to him, "What is it? What's going on?" But Al doesn't answer. The door opens and there's this big, tough-looking guy with a black beard. They can see a light inside. Al says, "Is Freddie here?"

The guy has this thick foreign accent. He says, "Who wans ta know?"

Al says, "I'm Al Croppe. C-r-o-p-p-e. Croppe. Sid General sent me."

The guy says, "Wha' chew wan'?"

Al says, "I wanna talk to Freddie. Is Freddie here?"

The guy hits himself on the chest like a gorilla and he says, "I Freddie. Wha' chew wan'?"

Al says, "My friend here needs some clothes."

Freddie looks at Dave. It's so dark he probably can't see him out there but he says, "Okay. You come in."

They go in the basement and there's not much light but they can see that the place is jammed to the walls with clothes hanging on long racks made of galvanized pipe. It looks like the biggest rummage sale in history. Except it's all new stuff. They got everything. The stuff is squeezed in so tight that if you pull something off a rack the stuff on either side of it comes off. There's piles of stuff in the corners—shoe boxes, shirts in plastic bags, underwear, socks, everything—it's piled chest high. Things all over the floor. You step on them when you walk. There's suits and ties on the floor between the racks and they just leave them there so when you go down the aisles you get them tangled up in your feet. The light is so bad you can't be sure what colors you're looking at. Al goes right to work pulling suits off the racks. "What size you take, Dave?" he says. "My friend here needs a couple of complete outfits," he says to Freddie. "He's gonna need a suitcase too. You got luggage?"

Freddie goes over and sits on a table and watches them. He says, "We got evrating."

Al picks out two suits, two sport jackets, and four pair of pants. "Grab some shirts off that pile," he says.

"Whad color you wan'?" Freddie says. "Here. Take. Take dis. How many you wan'?" And he starts tossing shirts onto a table. Every time he takes one off the pile some of the other shirts slide down to the floor.

"Ties," Al says.

Freddie says, "Ties, belts, socks. You need undawear? Take undawear."

Al picks out a big suitcase and says to Dave, "Pack all this shit up and I'll take care of the man here. How much you want for this shit."

Freddie says, "Two hawnert." And he holds up these two

fat fingers that look like white carrots with the dirt still on them.

Al laughs. He says, "Be serious, man. We're in a hurry."

"Two hawnert," Freddie says and he's waving his fat fingers.

Al says, "Is the boss in? I think you got me mixed up with somebody else. You're giving me the retail price."

"The boss ain 'ere," Freddie says. "I make da prize."

Al says, "Look, Freddie, the boss knows me. He's not gonna like you rippin' me off."

"Two hawnert," Freddie says.

Al says, "Listen, man, I gotta tell you something. I like you and I'm gonna be straight with you. I can see you're not the kind of guy that anybody pushes around. So I'm going to let you in on something. This place is known. You know what I mean? That's why they leave you here by yourself. One of these days this place is gonna get hit. Look at all this shit. You get caught with all this in here and you won't get any money. You'll get time. You understand me? You know what I'm talkin' about? They're settin' you up, man. Look, I'm talkin' to you straight because I like you. I like the way you handle yourself. You don't let nobody push you around. Now listen to me. I'm going to do something for you. I don't want to see you take a rap for somebody else. I got people in this business, the retail end, and I'm gonna send them down here to buy you out. The whole thing. They'll pay your price. You understand me? You get yours, the boss gets his. I'm gonna do that because I like you. I'll give you a phone number you can call to set it up. Now this stuff, what I got here, this is nothing. This is peanuts. Small potatoes in an operation like you're running. Am I right? One suitcase. You won't even notice it."

Freddie holds up his two fat fingers again and says, "Two hawnert. And don't give me bullshit."

Al says, "I'll tell you what I'll do. I'll give you twenty-five. That's for yourself because you're tough. You're a tough man, Freddie. I give you credit. You don't back down. I like that. I'll tell you what I'm gonna do for you. If you ever need a job, you look me up. Al Croppe. C-r-o-p-p-e."

"All righ'," Freddie says. "You big bullshit but I come down. One hawnert."

"For Chrissakes, man!" Al says. "What's the matter with you? I'm offering you twenty-five for yourself. Money in your pocket. The boss doesn't know if two suits are missing. He doesn't care. He expects you to make something for yourself. You want to lose his respect? You got to let people know you take care of yourself."

"One hawnert," Freddie says.

Al says, "One hawnert, your ass. I can get it retail at that price. I can go to Macy's and buy it for that. Let's be serious. Let's do business. You and me. You want to do business for your boss, then go get a job at Macy's. You work here, man, and you got to stand up for yourself. You understand me? You and your boss, that's oil and water. He's lookin' out for number one. That's what you got to do. I'll give you fifty dollars for yourself."

Freddie looks around. He gets down off the table and comes over to Al like he doesn't want anybody to hear and he says, "All righ'. Fifty dolla'. Take da stuff."

Al takes out a twenty-dollar bill and hands it to him and starts heading for the door. He says, "Dave, get the luggage and let's go."

Freddie says, "Hey! Wha' you doin'? Thirty dolla' more. You gimmie thirty dolla' more."

Al says, "Hey, Freddie, I'm bein' nice. What are you tryin' to pull on me? I'm a wholesale customer. I told you Sid General sent me. Why do you keep talking retail? Fifty dollars, that's retail. I put the wholesale price right in your hand. You got any complaints, talk to Sid. Let's go, Dave."

"You don' go nowhere," Freddie says. "You bullshit."

Al's disgusted now. He says, "Dave, you got thirty dollars on you? Give him thirty dollars and shut him up."

Winger's got plenty of money. He's got the money from the Blitnis job and the Dellawood job but he doesn't want to give it away. But he's scared. He doesn't know who these guys are and he wants to get out of there so he gives Freddie thirty dollars and they leave.

When they're outside he says to Al, "What kind of place was that?"

Al says, "Immigrants. You know the kind of stuff they do. Hole-in-the-wall. In twenty years he'll own a department store. He'll drive Macy's out of business. Those bastards are taking over the country."

Dave says, "That's no store."

Al says, "Hey, kid, you're smart. You're a college boy. So act it. If you don't know, don't ask."

They get a cab and Croppe takes him home. Dave doesn't

like this. Now he sees he made a mistake. But he doesn't know how to handle it.

He gets out of the cab with the suitcase and Al says to him, "Hey, don't look so sad. We got a good price for that stuff. The suitcase alone is worth fifty bucks. Don't worry about it. That's a good place to shop. We'll go back there one of these days and get you a whole wardrobe."

IF I HAD MY WISH, DAVE WOULD HAVE LEFT THAT suitcase in the cab with Al and said, "Forget it. I made a mistake." The man is a shark and Dave Winger was in no way prepared to deal with him. Dave was a naive kid, a babe in the woods. He should have apologized—just to get out of that car and get away from Al Croppe. "I'm sorry. I won't sign for a loan. I won't go to the bank. I'm out of this."

As much as I liked having him around here painting apartments for the senile population, I wish he went back to Ohio before he got involved with Al Croppe. The best thing would be if he had packed up that morning and I never saw or heard of him again. I knew what would happen once he went back to Ohio. Back there he's just like the rest of his kind. I wouldn't trust any one of them with a ten-foot pole. Once he's back in Ohio, I know what he's doing. He'll sit in the country club and tell stories about how he did charity work for the lower elements in Queens, New York. But what he says out in Ohio I don't hear. So I don't care.

And why should I care what Dave Winger does wherever he is? Why should I care and get involved if he's mixed up with a con artist like Al Croppe? It's no skin off my nose. Why should I even have an opinion? I'll tell you why. Because I liked Dave Winger. He was different. He wasn't always out for the buck. At least he wasn't back then. I know I was always knocking him and trying to show he was a hypocrite or that he was a rich boy playacting but I liked him for what he was doing. Even if it was an act, he was still helping people out and not trying to make money from them. He was not trying to squeeze anybody. He wasn't living for money.

I look around myself and what do I see? I'm in the Green Leaf and here's Max, the bartender. Now Max is a nice guy. He's a good bartender. I like him. You go in and talk to him and he'll give you a sympathetic ear. What you tell him will stay with him. He don't gossip. But on the other hand, I trust him only so far. If you're a good bartender you're friendly with everybody. But you're not everybody's friend. Say I got a problem with Al Croppe. I'm not going to discuss that with Max because I know that when Al Croppe comes to pay his tab he'll lay down an extra fifty dollars for Max. I leave a tip on the bar when I drink but it'll take a long time before my tips add up to fifty dollars. So as much as I like Max and as much as I trust him and no matter how friendly we are, I know what makes the world go round and I know which side Max's bread is buttered on.

But I don't have to talk about Max. I could talk about anybody. I could talk about myself. Do I eat shit for a two-dollar tip? I do. I smile at the customers and talk nice and carry suitcases and listen to all kinds of garbage and sympathize with everybody who sits in the back seat as if they were the best people in the world. And what do I get out of it? The difference between that fake smile and looking at people straight and telling them what I really think is maybe five dollars a day. Some days more, some days less. But that's twenty-five dollars a week and I can't afford to give it up just so I can enjoy myself by giving out honest opinions. When you deal with the public, you do not get bonuses for honesty. What you need is a smile.

But to get back to Dave Winger—once he went along with Al's deal, once he got involved in it, all that idealism went out the window for good. But I'll say this for him—he didn't throw it out just like that. He tried to get away from Al. The trouble was he was a baby. He was naive. Maybe he was weak. He was like a fly in a spider web. He knows he's got to get out of the web if he wants to survive but he just can't do it.

So the next morning, after they bought the clothes, when Al comes to take him to the bank Dave is not dressed in his new suit. Dave says to him, "I changed my mind. I can't go to the bank."

Al is dressed like a millionaire. His pants have creases so sharp they look like metal. He looks around. Winger's room is cheap. Old furniture. What people left out on the curb for the garbage pickup. Al sits down. He says, "Get dressed. I'll wait."

Dave says, "I don't like the way things are going."

Al says, "What things?"

Dave says, "Everything."

Al says, "For instance?"

Dave says, "I don't like that place last night. And I don't feel like I know what's going on."

Al says, "Nothing's going on. What do you want to know? Ask me. I got no secrets. We're partners."

Dave says, "I just don't like it. I don't feel comfortable with what's happening."

Al says, "You don't feel comfortable? What kind of talk is that? This is business, not a vacation. When you take a vacation you feel comfortable. In business you work. Work is not comfortable. It's a strain. You make commitments and you got to deliver. You gave me your word. I made commitments on that. I don't back out on my commitments. A man's word is his bond. It's a contract. It's a matter of honor."

Dave says, "I don't like what happened last night."

Al says, "Nothing happened last night."

Dave says, "I mean that guy Freddie. The whole deal. That place didn't look right."

Al says, "I'll tell you something, Dave. You're gonna run

into a lot of different people in business. Strange people. People with strange names. People who don't shave. People who don't take baths. But in business the only thing that counts is the dollar. A guy offers you a good price—you take it. You don't ask questions. It's a democracy. That scares a lot of people. They're not used to democracy. I'm lookin' at you now and I see a scared kid. Am I right?"

Dave says, "I'm not scared. I just think maybe I'm in over my head."

Al says, "You took the words out of my mouth. You feel like you're in over your head. That says it all. But that's why I'm here. I've been through all this. I'm your guide. We're on a boat and we're setting out on the sea of commerce. Sometimes the sea is rough but you don't get off the boat in the middle of the water. You'd drown. Then you'd definitely be in over your head. You stay on the boat until you come to dry land. Now, I would like to continue talking because you have a lot to learn and I feel it's my duty to teach you. But not right now because the first rule of business, Dave, is 'Time is money.' Just sitting here and talking is costing us money. I got a chauffeur and a limo downstairs and the man has to be paid by the hour so let's not sit here talking because it runs up the bill."

"You rented a limousine?" Dave says.

Al says, "When you go to the bank for a loan, what counts most is the impression you make. What they see. That's why when I go to the bank I travel first class."

Dave says, "How much does a limousine cost?"

Al says, "A thousand dollars an hour."

Dave almost has a heart attack. He's speechless. He doesn't know whether this guy is serious or joking. And he's afraid to ask who's paying for it.

Al says to him, "Relax. I'm not here to eat you up. I'm on your side. I know why you're nervous. Let's be honest. You're nervous because you don't understand me. Am I right? You haven't done business with entrepen-ewers before so you think I deal with shady people, like Freddie, and I rent limousines when you'd take a taxi or the bus. This is no good, Dave. You got to realize that I'm an experienced businessman and you're only a virgin. You're like a boy on his first visit to the whorehouse. Maybe you talked a little too big and now you're afraid to go. But we made an agreement and we're partners. We got to trust each other. If you don't trust me, that's very insulting. That means you're questioning my word, my experience, my knowledge—everything. I could take that as an insult. But I want you to know that I don't. I like you and I know, in your heart, that you are a nice kid and you don't mean to be insulting. You're just scared. You don't know banks. You don't have experience. But that's why I'm here. I'm here to protect your interests. My job is to make sure you don't get taken in. We're partners. What affects you affects me. We're in the same boat. If you get cheated, I get cheated. And you know me. I'm not going to get cheated. You understand?"

Dave is alone up there in his room with Al Croppe and he needs help but there is nobody who's going to help him. He sees he can't get out of this so he's desperate. When you get desperate like that sometimes your mind stops working right and you start to think you see a way out where there isn't one. Dave starts to figure that the bank will never give him a loan. He's got no collateral. The only thing he's got is Al Croppe's word and the bank is never going to take that. So he figures maybe it's safe to go. The bank will turn him down and that will be the end of the deal. And if by some crazy chance the bank does take Al's word, then that has to mean they know him and Al is telling the truth and he really is a legitimate businessman. If that's true, Dave has nothing to worry about. So either way he's okay.

So he gets dressed in a suit and tie and they go downstairs and there is Sid General and his limousine. He's wearing a gray suit like a chauffeur and a chauffeur's cap. I don't know if Al hired him, like he said to Dave, or if Sid is doing him a favor, or if they got some kind of percentage arrangement. Nobody knows what goes on between them and nobody will ever know.

Sid says to them, "Where you been? I'm waiting half an hour."

Al says, "The kid here is a careful dresser. Long time in front of the mirror."

Sid and Al laugh, which makes Dave feel uncomfortable, like they're making fun of him or they got some kind of joke behind his back.

It's a very plush car. There's a bar, a telephone, a little TV, and it rides smooth like a boat. Al turns on the TV to some game show and tells Dave to relax. Dave can't relax. He can't follow the program. Al is having a good time. He's yelling out the answers to the questions before the contestants can.

Sid drives up Queens Boulevard, stops in front of a bank, and parks at a hydrant. Al says, "Let's go," and he's out of the car, heading for the bank. Dave gets out and goes after him. He catches up to him inside just as Al is walking up to one of the people at the desks. He says, "I'm looking for Mr. Rollins," and he's pulling off his gloves, one finger at a time, like some European baron. The woman at the desk calls Mr. Rollins and a skinny guy with a mustache comes out and says, "Gentlemen, what can I do for you?"

Al says, "Mr. Rollins. Glad to meet you. Albert T. Croppe. C-r-o-p-p-e. Croppe. Jim Brooks told me you're the man in Queens to see. This is Mr. Winger. Mr. Winger, Mr. Rollins. Do you have an office where we can talk?"

Rollins looks like he's not sure what's happening but he leads them to the back where he's got a little office. Al sits down and makes himself comfortable. He says, "Did Jim call you?"

Rollins doesn't know what he's talking about. "Jim?" he says.

"Jim Brooks," Al says. "Am I in the right bank?" And he looks around like he's trying to see where he is. He says, "Jim Brooks. Chairman of the board."

"Oh! Oh, of course," Rollins says. "Mr. Brooks. Of course you're in the right bank."

Al says, "I was starting to wonder. Did he call you?"

Rollins says, "Mr. Brooks?"

Al says, "Yes, yes, Mr. Brooks. Jim Brooks. What's going on here? Dave, go out and tell Sidney we'll be longer than I expected. We're at a hydrant, Mr. Rollins. Can you see it from your window? Will I get a ticket there? I have a fetish about traffic tickets. I don't like to pay them, Mr. Rollins. It's a small thing but I don't like to pay them. Would you take a look out the window? The gray car." Rollins takes a look and sees the limo.

He says, "I don't think you'll get a ticket as long as your driver is in the car."

"All right," Al says. "David, tell Sidney we'll be a while."

Dave goes out. When he gets there Sid is sleeping. Sid is not the kind of guy you want to disturb or tap on the sleeve so Dave is calling him in this little voice, "Sid . . . Sid." But Sid is sound asleep. Finally he touches him on the arm and Sid jumps. Dave almost drops dead. He thought Sid was going to pull a gun and blow him away. By the time Dave recovers, Sid is smiling at him and he says, "What is it, kid?"

Dave says, "Al told me to tell you we'd be longer than he thought."

Sid says, "It's very thoughtful of you to come out and tell me that."

Dave has the feeling that Sid is laughing at him again but what can he do?

He goes back in and when he gets to Rollins's office Al is talking and Rollins looks very nervous. Al says, "Ah, here's David. David, we decided on a fifty-thousand-dollar loan. Mr. Rollins is going to get the papers now."

Dave wants to ask why fifty thousand. Al told him twenty-five. But he's afraid to talk in front of Rollins. When Rollins goes out to get the papers, Dave says, "What's going on?"

Al says, "Dave, we're in the bank and we're arranging for a loan to start our business, David Winger Home Repair. You know that. Mr. Rollins is getting the papers and writing us a check. We had a nice talk, Mr. Rollins and me. He's very interested that we should succeed. All these people want us to succeed. That should make you feel good."

Well this is not what Dave asked. What Dave really wants to know, what he can't believe, is why this banker is out there writing a check—for any amount of money. This whole deal is so strange that Dave can't believe he's doing it. But the explanation is very simple. It's Al Croppe. The man has an instinct. He knows people. He knows how to talk to people. In this case, he sent Dave out to see Sid General, so Dave don't hear what goes on at the crucial point. But look at the situation. He put the guy in a spot where he either gives them a check for fifty thousand dollars or else he's got to call the chairman of the board of the bank at home on a private number. And this is not the kind of guy who will do that. And Al knew it. I would bet Al never laid eyes on the guy before but he sized him up exactly just by talking to him for a few minutes. That's what I mean by instinct. It's not brains because Al is not all that smart. Of course it takes more than instinct to do this. It also takes a lot of nerve.

Now Dave, who is a lot smarter than Al, can't handle Al because he don't have that instinct or the nerve. So Al is running circles around him and Dave is so scared he can't think straight. He's trying. He's trying to figure out what's going on. He says to Al, "Who is this guy Brooks?"

Al is calm. He says, "Mr. Brooks is chairman of the board of the bank. Jim Brooks."

Dave says, "How do you know him?"

Al points to an air vent and he says, "Don't talk now. The place is wired."

So the two of them sit there for a couple of minutes. Dave knows the place isn't wired. He knows it's an air vent but he's so bamboozled he can't think straight. After a couple of minutes he gets a hold of himself and says, "What did you say to him when I was outside?"

Al says, "I gave him our sales pitch. You know the shpiel. Discounts. Golden reputation. Known all over. Jackson Heights, Woodside, Elmhurst. I'm talking you up, Dave. We're in it together. If you do good, I do good. Ah, here's Mr. Rollins. We're going to make Mr. Rollins very happy, aren't we, Dave?"

Rollins is carrying a bunch of papers and a check. He lays the papers down on the desk, one beside the other. Winger can't remember how many there are but it seems like a dozen, and he has to sign them all. Then Al picks up the check, which is made out to David Winger for fifty thousand dollars, and the next thing Winger knows they're back in the car and Sid is cruising on Queens Boulevard.

Dave has so many questions he can't get them arranged in his mind. He says, "What did you say to him when I was outside?"

Al says, "I told him I'm a friend of Sid General," and Sid and Al both start to laugh.

9

THEY DROP HIM OFF AND WINGER GOES UP TO HIS room and lays down. It's the middle of the day but he's exhausted because he hardly slept the night before. Then, all of a sudden, he sits up in bed like a shot. He doesn't have the check! Croppe has it. He can't believe he's so stupid. He never even thought about that check. Fifty thousand dollars and he didn't pay attention to where it was. He gets up, changes into his regular clothes, and goes down to the Green Leaf. He tells Max he has to get in touch with Al Croppe. Max says he'll give him a message if he should happen to see him. Dave says, "I got to see him soon. It's very important."

Max shakes his head. He says, "If I see him, I'll tell him." Meanwhile Max gives him some slips of paper with names and phone numbers.

He puts the papers in his pocket and goes out. He can't think about making calls and giving estimates. All he can think about is that he just signed a bank note for fifty thousand dollars and gave away the check. He starts walking around the streets because he can't sit still. He goes down Roosevelt to Queens Boulevard, back up to Roosevelt, and then to Northern Boulevard. He's walking for hours. It's cold. There's still snow on the ground, but by now it's turned black.

All afternoon he feels like he's going nuts. Just for something to do he calls one of the numbers and walks over to give the people an estimate. He's so desperate from thinking about money by then that he gives them a high estimate. He gives such a high estimate that they look at him like he's crazy. They don't even complain. The guy laughs and says something about a misunderstanding.

It gets dark and he goes home. He never even ate lunch or supper because he's so upset he didn't get hungry. All of a sudden the doorbell rings. He goes downstairs, opens the door, and it's Al Croppe.

As soon as he sees Croppe he thinks he's saved. He was afraid Al took the fifty thousand and disappeared. He was afraid he'd never see him again. But here is Al coming to look for him. He's so relieved he feels like he loves the guy.

Al comes in laughing and acting buddy-buddy. "Hey, Dave," he says, "you're more trouble than you're worth. You never took the check. Do you know that?"

Does he know that? He's laughing now. He says, "I know.
I forgot. I've been looking for you all afternoon."

Al says, "You're lucky you got me for a partner. I took
care of everything. This could have been a real mess."

Dave says, "What happened? Do you have the check?"

Al says, "Listen to this. I went to see my lawyer, Donnie
Grenlily. You ever hear of him? A very well-known lawyer.
A top guy. Sharp, sharp, sharp. I wanted him to draw up our
partnership papers. I figured you had the check and you'd
take care of depositing it. So I call Donnie and Donnie's
secretary tells me he's at the tennis club on Vernon Boulevard. I go over there and we sit down and have drinks and
I'm telling him about the partnership and I reach into this
pocket and what do I come out with but your check. You got
no phone. It's two o'clock and there's no way I can contact
you. The banks close in one hour. So what am I going to do?
I'm not going to walk around with a fifty-thousand-dollar
check in my pocket overnight. What if I lose it? So I say to
Donnie, 'Donnie, what do I do?' He says, 'Al, you've got to
deposit it.' I say, 'How can I? The check is made out to David
Winger and he's got no account. I can't sign his name and
put it into my account.' He says, 'Go in and open an account
in his name.' I say, 'Donnie, I can't do that. They want all
that information, Social Security, mother's maiden name.'
He says, 'What's the alternative? You want to walk around
all night with the kid's fifty thousand in your pocket? Somebody hits you on the head and it's gone. *Phffft.* Just like that.
And who's on the line for it? Who's going to have to pay?
Not you. That kid that's just trying to start out in life. Al, go

in there and deposit that check. Sign David Winger and make up any information you need.' So that's what I did. So now you have a checking account for fifty thousand dollars. I had to make up a Social Security number, your mother's maiden name, and all that kind of stuff. But that doesn't matter. The only problem now is that it's in my handwriting. That means if you sign checks, they're no good. That's what we've got to straighten out."

Dave says, "Let's go down there tomorrow morning and tell them."

Al says, "Tell them what?"

Dave says, "Tell them it was an emergency and let's get the money out of there."

Al says, "You want me to go into a federal bank and tell them I opened an account, signed somebody else's name, gave false information, made up a fake Social Security number, and that now I want to take the money out? You must be kidding. I tell them that and they're not gonna give me money. They're gonna call the FBI. We can't do that."

Dave says, "Then what can we do?"

Al says, "That's just what I said to Grenlily. I said, 'Donnie, how am I gonna get the money out of there?' You see, when I came out of that bank I was so relieved to have the money in a safe place that at first I didn't realize what I did. But by the time I got back to the tennis club I was shaking. Let me tell you I was scared. I am not accustomed to lying to the authorities like that and, on top of that, putting it on paper. I interrupted his tennis game and I said, 'Donnie, you got me into this, how am I gonna get out of it?'

"Dave, I hope you realize that you can't go in there either. If I write a check to Dave Winger or to 'Cash' they'd ask you for ID. They won't cash a check like that without ID. If you show an ID that says David Winger with a different signature and different information all hell will break loose. You understand me? So I said to Donnie, 'You got to help me out.' Donnie looks at me and says, 'Why are you so excited?' He says, 'Don't worry. You think you're the only one this ever happened to? There's a standard procedure for this.' And he explains it to me. First of all, do you have a valid ID?"

Dave shows him some ID and Al says, "Good. Now we got to do what is called laundering the money. Sometimes this is done crookedly but what we're doing is honest. It's totally legal and aboveboard because we're not trying to hide this money or steal it from anybody. We're just trying to straighten out a misunderstanding. So here's what we have to do. First of all I'm gonna get Sid General to give you a lift to Atlantic City in his limousine. Now wait a minute! Let me finish. The reason for Atlantic City is because in Atlantic City fifty thousand dollars is peanuts and they won't make a fuss. Sid will take you to a hotel. Use your ID, take a room, sign for it. Everything just the way you would normally do. This is entirely on the up and up, straight and honest, so you don't have to hide anything. Sign for your room and tell them you want to establish fifty thousand dollars credit. Tell them you're staying five days and you need ten thousand a day. That sounds like a lot but, believe me, down there it's nothing. They'll look at your ID, fill out a form, and then they'll run a credit check. They ask your bank if you can cover fifty thousand. The bank will tell them yes because you've got the fifty thousand deposited in your name. So now everything is set. I write out checks before you go. I pre-date these checks and sign them with your name, in my handwriting, just the way I signed at the bank, so when the bank sees it, they'll accept it because that's the way they have your signature. You understand? What I'll do is write out check number two, number four, number six, number eight, and number ten. That's five checks, ten thousand dollars each, one a day. I'll leave the 'Pay To' line blank. When you go down to the cashier's window, you've got check number one on top. It's blank. Right? You fill it out. You leave the 'Pay To' line blank and say to the cashier, 'You got a stamp or shall I fill that out?' He says, 'I got a stamp.' So you leave it blank. And it's blank on check number two, the one I wrote. Now you fill out check number one right in front of him. He sees you do it. But you pick up the checkbook and instead of tearing out number one, you tear out number two. You follow me? He can't see which one you're tearing out because you're holding the book up. You give him check number two, which I made out, he stamps the hotel's name on the 'Pay To' line, and asks you how you want the cash. You do this for five days and you got fifty thousand dollars. The hotel deposits the checks, the bank pays the hotel, and everybody's happy. The hotel does you a service and in exchange you stay there and pay for room and board for five days and gamble a little, which means they come out ahead. Everybody wins and we get out of a tight spot. Get yourself a safe deposit box in a bank down there and put the cash in it until you have it all. And that's it. What it amounts to is a nice vacation."

Dave says, "I don't like it."

Al says, "I knew you wouldn't. I said to myself, this sounds like fun. Dave won't like it. So if you got a different plan, I'll be glad to listen."

Dave says, "I don't know. But there has to be a better way. Can't you make out a check for fifty thousand dollars to somebody we trust, sign my name, and let him give us the money?"

Al says, "Look, you are now talking about big money, enough to set somebody up for a nice few years to live comfortably. I don't know anybody who can deposit a check like that and get cash right away. It'll have to sit there till it clears. That can take a week. There is nobody that I would give away fifty thousand to for a week on his word alone. It's too much. And nobody's going to sign an IOU because he doesn't know if the check is going to bounce."

Dave says, "We can make the IOU contingent on the check being good."

Al says, "Contingent! What is contingent? This is business. You don't do contingent in business. It's yes or no. You start with funny words and people don't trust you. Now look, this is the way my lawyer told me to do it. He said it's done all the time. The hotels know people do it and they like it. It's more rooms rented. It's gambling money. I got the checkbooks right here. You want them or not?"

Dave looks at the checks and says, "These have the wrong address."

Al says, "I told you I had to make up all that stuff. I couldn't remember your address and I couldn't stand there thinking about it when they asked me so I just said the first thing that came to mind."

Dave says, "How come you got them printed already?"

Al says, "They have a machine right there. I'll take you down there if you want to see it. Go down there yourself. It's on Vernon Boulevard near the tennis club."

Dave says, "Isn't there some other way we can do this?"

Al says, "Not if you want to do it legal."

So the next morning Sid picks him up and drives him to Atlantic City.

10

I'VE BEEN TO ATLANTIC CITY. I TOOK MY WIFE. I couldn't picture Brenda in a gambling joint. I still can't. I picture Brenda at home, watching television. She was excited that day. I looked at her sitting next to me on the bus and I felt sorry for her. She had on this gray suit that must have been fifteen years old even at that time. I said to her, "Brenda, I don't feel like gambling. I'm just gonna find myself a seat and relax. Here's twenty dollars. See how you do."

I could see she was disappointed. She tried to get me to come with her but I wouldn't. So she went her way and I went mine. It didn't take her long to lose the twenty dollars and then she walked on the boardwalk and sat around by herself until it was time to get on the bus.

I went to a hotel, had lunch, a couple of beers, read the paper, relaxed, and watched the people. I don't need to gamble. I can take it or leave it because I know that gambling is all fixed. In a casino the odds are fixed in favor of the house. At the track, the horses are drugged. In sports, basketball teams shave points, in football they miss the spread, in baseball they throw games. The only way to win is if you have inside information. Otherwise you're throwing your money away.

Let me tell you what the psychology is in Atlantic City. First of all the games are fixed in favor of the house. They want you to gamble because the more you gamble, the more they win. So they arrange everything to put you in the mood. Everything is made of red, gold, and silver. Expensive colors. And everything is plush. They want you to feel like there's an ocean of money out there and all you got to do is guess the right number or put a quarter in the right slot and waves of dollar bills are going to break over your head. One bet will change your life. Maybe your next bet. So you got to keep betting. And all the time you're betting you feel that ocean of money rolling and rolling all around the casino.

In the limo on the way down Sid General says to Winger, "The only reason these hotels give you credit is so you can gamble. I guess Al explained that. You got to go in the casino every day and invest at least a thousand dollars. Even that's cutting it close for a guy they're giving ten thousand dollars' credit. You got to do at least a thousand a day in the casino or they'll stop cashing your checks."

Well, Dave doesn't want to gamble. Not a thousand a day. This is money he's got to pay back to the bank. But by now this is just one more thing. He feels like he's in quicksand and everything he does gets him in deeper.

It's a long trip to Atlantic City and Sid doesn't say much but every once in a while he opens up his mouth and gives Dave another piece of advice which makes things worse and makes Dave more nervous. He says to him, "When you cash the check, do it at the same time every day. That way you always see the same cashier. It'll save you trouble later on. And he won't bother you with questions."

Finally they get to Atlantic City and Sid drives him to a hotel. Who decided which hotel and how they decided, Dave has no idea. Sid is wearing his gray chauffeur's cap and a gray suit and naturally, with that limo, they make a good impression. Sid opens the door for him and takes his suitcases out of the trunk. He leaves the stuff on the sidewalk for the guys from the hotel and drives away. Winger is alone. He's standing there in the middle of the cold—don't forget it's winter—and he's out on the sidewalk, near the beach, and everything is bare and dead. He's stranded. He's even afraid to go in and register. But—surprise!—everything goes very nicely. No fuss. ID, registration, credit check, no problems. And in the morning they cash his check. Ten thousand dollars. He handles it like a pro. He walks a couple of blocks to a bank, gets a safe deposit box, puts in nine thousand dollars, and with the rest he's got plenty for eating, drinking, and gambling.

Let me tell you, you can get used to that situation. It's not hard to take. Two, three days go by and he's playing roulette and blowing his full quota, a thousand dollars a day, eating nicely, sleeping in a nice room, no problems. It's lucky he's a sensible kid because you could lose your head and blow everything you have. This kind of thing is like fever. That's why they have Gambler's Anonymous. He makes sure he puts that nine thousand in the safe deposit box first so he's not tempted to bet more than a thousand a day.

The third day he hits a hot streak at the roulette table and wins over three thousand dollars. But by then three thousand doesn't seem like so much. He works all week for three hundred fifty or at the most five hundred bucks, from which he has to take out his expenses, and here he is laying one thousand dollars' worth of chips on the table in one night, twenty dollars a chip, and a chip doesn't feel like anything. That's how fast you get used to it. And once you win you feel like you can always win. You feel like the next number you pick has got to be a winner. Then you have to bet because if you've got a number in your head—and you always have a number in your head—you think it's got to win so if you don't bet it you'll miss out. So Winger wins three thousand and keeps betting and before you know it he loses it all back plus the thousand he started with.

Another thing he gets used to very fast is the luxury, the respect, the people calling him sir. Waitresses bring him drinks on the house. The pit boss gives him a comp meal. He tosses a chip to the dealer and the guy calls him sir. It feels good. This is more like how he grew up. He didn't realize how much humiliation he was taking—not from other people but from himself, in his own mind, because he don't respect the work he's doing. He grew up respecting guys who work in suits with briefcases, professors, lawyers, businessmen, guys in suits, not guys who come home tired and dirty. The fourth day comes. He cashes his check. He puts nine thousand in the safe deposit box. He's got thirty-six thousand in there now. Enough to start a business. And that's what got him into this thing in the first place. But he hasn't been thinking about the business because he really got into this because of a girl, not because of a business. But now he's got the money and he realizes he better start to think about this business—David Winger Home Repair. He goes for a walk and tries to make plans in his head but he can't do it. First of all he doesn't really know what plans to make and second of all he doesn't even want to do it. When it comes down to it, he doesn't want to be in this kind of business. It's cold so he goes in and has lunch and then he buys some magazines and goes up to his room to relax.

He's up in his room and the phone rings. Right away this makes him nervous. He picks it up and it's Croppe. "Hey, Dave! How ya doin'?"

"What's wrong?" he says.

Al says, "What makes you think something's wrong?"

Dave says, "What are you calling about?"

Al says, "I want to see how you're doing. How is everything?"

Dave says, "It's fine. It's going according to plan."

Al says, "That's great. That's really great. I'm glad to hear it. I knew you'd be okay. I got a lot of faith in you. Listen,

Dave, can you do me a favor? Go out to a phone booth, out on the street somewhere, not in the hotel, and call this number." And he gives him a phone number. "Wait till three o'clock," he says. "That'll give you time."

Dave says, "What's this about?"

Al says, "You'll hear when you call."

Around 2:30 he gets a bunch of change and goes out and finds a phone booth. At three o'clock he dials the number. Al picks it up. Dave can hear street noises so he knows Al must also be in a phone booth out on a street and from the area code he knows Al is still in New York. Al says, "Listen, Dave, don't get nervous but we may have a little problem."

Naturally that makes him nervous right away. He says, "What's the matter?"

Al says, "Tomorrow morning go down and cash the check the way you always do and put the money in the safe deposit box. Then mail me the key. If you don't trust me, mail it to a friend or somebody you trust, but don't keep it and don't mail it to yourself. Then make sure you got nothing on you that could tell anybody that searches you or your room that you rented this box. Receipts, notes to yourself, anything—get rid of it. Then take all the checks you got left over and get rid of them too. Get rid of the pen. Everything you got that you used on the checks, get rid of it. And don't throw it in a wastebasket in your room or in the hotel. Throw it where nobody's ever going to find it, so nobody could ever tell you wrote those checks. You understand? Something happened up here and that stuff could be evidence against you. Get rid of it without any trace and you're okay. Then just sit tight. I'm going to give you Donnie Gren-lily's phone number. If there's any problem, call him right away. But whatever you do, don't say anything to anybody. You're in the clear as long as you don't say anything. We might have a problem but we can handle it if you don't talk. I'm going to be very straight with you. Your ass is on the line and if you talk you may end up in jail. So let Donnie do the talking. If anybody asks you anything, even if it's the po-lice—especially the police—don't trust anybody. Nobody's your friend down there except me and Donnie. Anybody asks you anything, say, 'Talk to my lawyer.' "

You can imagine what this does to Dave. He says, "Al, what happened? What's this all about?"

Al says, "It's very hard to explain over the phone. Just do what I told you. Then, tomorrow morning, after you take care of everything, after you put the cash in the box, mail the key, get rid of the checkbook, the pen, and everything else, call me at this number. I'll be here waiting for your call. Ten-thirty tomorrow morning. There's no point in talking before that."

Dave says, "You've got to tell me what's happening."

Al says, "Tomorrow morning, ten-thirty," and he hangs up.

11

SO NOW DAVE IS A WRECK. IT'S A LITTLE AFTER three and he's got to get through the afternoon and the night and then cash his check in the morning before he can call Croppe at 10:30 to find out what's going on. He eats dinner and goes to the casino to do his gambling. There's one thing about gambling—when you have money on the line it holds your attention. You forget all your other troubles. So when Winger plays roulette that night and starts to win he doesn't know what else is happening in the world. For a few hours he forgets Croppe. He has a lucky night and he's winning for a long time. But, as I say, the odds are in favor of the house and if you gamble long enough you lose. So eventually he loses what he won plus his thousand but it takes him almost three hours. Then he goes to a bar and has a few drinks. Between the liquor and the excitement he gets through the night. But he's scared. He's really scared.

In the morning he goes down to the cashier to cash the check. The cashier gives him the ten thousand but this time Winger thinks the guy is suspicious. Whether he is or not I don't know because Winger is my only source for this and he was so scared by then that he was a little crazy.

He puts nine thousand in the safe deposit box and keeps a thousand. He doesn't have to gamble any more but he keeps the extra thousand to pay the hotel bill and anything else that comes up.

He takes the checkbook and the pen and goes looking for a place to dump them. Atlantic City has a lot of vacant lots where they tore down buildings so there's a lot of old wood and stuff that can burn. In the winter bums use this stuff to start fires to keep warm. Winger finds a little fire in a vacant lot where nobody's around and he throws in the checkbook and the pen.

The next thing he's got to do is mail the key. He doesn't trust Croppe so he's not going to send it to him. He figures that could be the whole gimmick—to scare him, make him mail the key, and then Croppe takes the money and sticks him with the bank bill. But if he can't mail it to himself or Croppe, who can he mail it to? Guess who! He mails it to me. That was an expression of trust and friendship I could have done without. He doesn't explain anything. He just writes that I should hold on to this key and not tell anybody about it. He doesn't say what it is. But I take one look at it and I know it's the key to a safe deposit box. I see the postmark is Atlantic City and that's the first I knew he was down there. Maybe I don't know what's going on but it's easy enough to figure out that it's not something good. So I'm not happy. Without asking me, he pulls me into a deal which I don't know what it's about. And I'm supposed to take this risk for him without any compensation.

Back in Atlantic City, 10:30 A.M. comes, he finds a phone booth and dials the number. Al picks it up.

"It's all done," Dave says.

Al says, "Good. Then we're safe."

Dave says, "Safe from what? What's going on?"

Al says, "Here's the story. Sometime today, the bank up here is going to get the first check you wrote and they're going to bounce it."

Dave says, "Why?"

Al says, "I don't know. I think it's got something to do with the signature. I can't ask questions because they'll get suspicious. But right now we're okay. Let me ask you something else. Who saw you cash those checks?"

Dave says, "Just the cashier."

Al says, "Are you sure?"

Dave says, "Unless somebody was passing by at the time. But I don't think they'd pay attention if they were. Sid told me to do it at the same time every day so it was always the same cashier. He's the only one who saw me."

Al says, "That's good. That's very good. That means we're going to come out of this clean. We're going to smell like a rose. Those checks, every one of them, were made out by me. Am I right?"

Dave says, "Yes."

Al says, "And the only guy in the world who saw you cash them, the only guy who can say you cashed them is that cashier. Am I right?"

Dave says, "Yes."

Al says, "Then it's your word against his. But don't you say anything. Donnie will talk. He's gonna take care of it. He's gonna say you didn't cash those checks. He's gonna say you didn't make them out. And that's true because we know who did make them out. You follow me?"

Dave says, "I follow you but I don't understand why the bank would bounce the checks."

Al says, "I agree with you. That's why I say never trust a bank. That's my motto. The way I see it, they're giving us a hard time and that means we don't have to bend over backwards to help them. We're not gonna tell them who made out those checks because of the way they're acting. It wouldn't help you if they knew and right now all I care about is what helps you. All of us, Sid, Donnie, me, all we're interested in right now is you—not the bank, not the hotel—you. We want to make sure that you come out of this clean. So what we're gonna do is, we're gonna ask them—Donnie's gonna ask them, because he's your lawyer—he's gonna ask the hotel, the police, whoever bothers you, if you didn't make out those checks and you didn't cash them, what have they got against you? You understand me? They got one eyewitness that says you cashed them and that's all the evidence they got, and one eyewitness won't stand up in court. It's your word against his. That means you're off the hook. You're off the hook if you mailed the key. Did you mail the key?"

Dave says, "I mailed it."

Al says, "Good. Then they can't say you got the money. So they got no evidence at all. Who'd you mail it to?"

Dave says, "Russ. You know Russ. The cabdriver I'm always talking to in the Green Leaf."

That's me. My name is Russ. It's not my favorite name but that's what my mother put on my birth certificate—Russell—which I personally would not name a child. But I'm stuck with it and you can't blame anybody for his name.

Al says, "I know who you mean." But Al is annoyed. He don't want me involved. Maybe he thinks I'll mess up his plans. But he can't yell at Dave because he needs Dave to concentrate on what he's doing so he takes it out on me instead. He says some nasty things which Dave later tells me about. I won't repeat them here and I'm not going to be nasty myself. All I'll say is that I earn my money honestly, which Al Croppe never did.

Al says to him, "Dave, from what you're telling me, the news is good. You're home free. But you got to stay down there because if you leave it'll look bad. You leave and they'll put out a thirteen-state alarm. That'll turn it into a mess. So keep it simple. Stay there and give them a chance to accuse you. If they do, call Donnie. He'll take care of everything. Maybe it'll take an extra day or so more than we planned, but you'll come home with all the money and you'll be out of this."

What can Dave do? He's got to do what Croppe tells him. He went this far, he can't turn around now. They got him. He's their puppet. He's Pinocchio. Only he's dumber than Pinocchio. Pinocchio knew what he was doing. You remember the story? He goes to look for Gepetto. That's his own decision. Winger can't make a decision. All he can do is wait for them to tell him what to do next. He's plenty mad but he don't let Croppe know that because he needs Croppe. He's scared and he's got nobody else to turn to.

He goes in for lunch but he can't eat. He takes a walk. It's cold but he keeps walking. Finally, just to do something, he goes back to the casino.

He's got a thousand dollars in his pocket which he needs for the hotel bill. He's not supposed to gamble any more. All the checks are cashed so there's no point to it. But he starts looking around. He walks over to a roulette table and sees this fat lady in a yellow dress and a black raincoat. She looks like one of those gypsy people who sit in a store with a sign that says "Reader and Adviser." This lady has one chip in her hand and it's a hundred-dollar chip. The reason he notices her is because of the way she's acting. She's fidgeting around like she's really nervous. She shuts her eyes and then all of a sudden puts down her one chip on black without looking at what she's doing—as if she's got the evil eye and if she looks at it, it'll be jinxed. She turns around and walks across the aisle and stands there with her back to the roulette table, her eyes closed, and she's praying. Black wins. It's an even bet so they give her another hundred-dollar chip. Now she's got two of them. She puts one in this flea-bitten pocketbook and she watches a couple more spins. Same thing. She's all nerves, she prays and then, all of a sudden, without letting her eyes look down at the table, puts the chip on black again. She walks across the aisle like before and prays with her back to the roulette table. Black hits again. They lay down another hundred-dollar chip. She picks them both up, puts one in her pocketbook, and holds on to the other one. Then the same thing—and she wins again. That's three.

Meanwhile, he's also watching another lady at this table. This one isn't winning a hundred dollars every few spins. This one is playing every spin and she's winning big. This is a very different article. She's got on a ton of makeup and a million little lines on her face and the lipstick is sweating into the lines and looks disgusting. She's got orange hair, purple nails, and she's wearing this ugly blue suit. I think it's called electric blue. She looks like a witch but from the way they're treating her you'd think she was a beauty queen. The reason is, naturally, this lady has a big wall of chips in front of her and she's betting and laying out tips all over the place. She takes chips in each hand and spreads them around at different places on the board and she wins something on every spin. When you win on a roulette number you win a lot. It's thirty-five to one if you got the winning number, it's sixteen to one if you got it on the line between two numbers and one of them wins, and eight to one if it's on the corner of four numbers and one of the four wins. This lady is laying chips everywhere, putting two or three in some places, five or six in others, and she's hitting. Every chip she's got is worth at least twenty dollars. With five chips on a winning number she gets five times thirty-five. You figure it out. With twenty-, fifty-, a hundred-dollar chips, that comes to a lot of money. Every time the croupier shoves chips at her, she takes a twenty-dollar chip and tosses it back to him. When the waitress brings her a drink, she lays a twenty-dollar chip on the tray. When they bring her cigarettes, another twenty-dollar chip. They're falling all over this lady. She thinks she's the queen bee. She's only queen for a day, for as long as the chips last, but she knows that too. That's how gamblers are.

Winger is watching these two ladies rake in the chips and it looks to him like this is a day when everybody is a winner. It looks to him like the roulette wheel is saying, "Play me! Play me! I'm hot." And when it's hot, he who hesitates misses out. It won't stay hot forever. But the lady with the orange hair is betting too many chips for him to follow her. He's got to go with the fat lady in the yellow dress. She's laying down one chip at a time, always on black. He can handle that. Other people are doing it too and they're winning with her. Winger keeps watching and there she goes again, another chip on black, the same routine, and she wins again. He doesn't know how many times she won but he knows she hasn't lost. The lady is magic.

He's got ten hundred-dollar bills in a roll in his pocket. He pulls out the roll, peels off one bill, and lays it down on the table. The croupier says something to him and Winger wants to ask him what he said because he didn't hear it. The reason he didn't hear is because, just as the croupier was talking, somebody behind him yelled out, "Mr. Winger! Mr. Winger!"

The fat lady in the yellow dress is putting her hundred-dollar chip on black again. He wants to get a chip and bet with her but some lady behind him is yelling, "Mr. Winger!" and he's discombobulated by it because he's got so much fear in his mind from the thing with Croppe that he shoves his hundred-dollar bill back in his pocket. He turns around and sees the lady waving her pocketbook and yelling, "Mr. Winger! Mr. Winger! What a surprise!"

The croupier says, "No more bets."

The lady yells at him, "What are you doing in Atlantic City? How about that Melody Watson! Twenty-four to one. Did you ever have a tip like that in your life?"

The croupier says, "Number two is the winner. Black." The fat lady in the yellow dress is picking up another hundred-dollar chip.

The lady waving the pocketbook is still yelling at him. "I never expected you for a gambler. What is it? Melody Watson put you in the chips and you come here to parlay? I used to do that myself. I know a gambler when I see one. But it's not smart, Mr. Winger. Don't do it. You'll only lose. Especially at roulette. Come away from here. Come with me. You can't win at roulette," and she's grabbing his arm and pulling him. "Come on," she says. "Harry's here. It's a senior citizen trip. I want to show Harry who's here." She's pulling him and he's looking back at the table. The fat lady in the black raincoat is putting her money down again. Everybody at the table is betting with her. The other lady is pulling him to the doors. He's holding back. He hears the croupier say black is the winner. The other woman pulls him out of the casino into this fancy hallway that leads to the hotel. An old guy is sitting on a red velour seat reading a paper. Winger knows these people but they got him so discombobulated, especially with him expecting to be arrested any minute, that he can't think of who they are.

"Harry," she says. "Look who I found."

Harry looks up from his paper but he's a little slow and for a minute he can't figure out who Winger is. The lady says, "Mr. Winger, stay away from roulette. It's bad odds. It's worse than slot machines. Blackjack is the game. In blackjack we all got an equal chance. Come with me and I'll show you some ropes."

Winger says, "No, thanks. I'm just looking around."

She says, "Don't kid me. I saw you with your money on the table. If I didn't stop you, you'd already be losing money over there. Listen. I'm doing you a favor. I'll show you blackjack."

Harry says, "Don't listen to her. If you don't want to gamble don't do it. Stay with me. You can find plenty of enjoyment just looking around. People come here, they see the gambling, they spell caution to the wind, and they go home poor. I say, don't jump in unless you know the temperature of the water. Mr. Winger, this is not just a gambling mecca. This is a sightseer's paradise. You got fine stores here. Each and every hotel is a beautiful edifice worth looking at. Sitting here is like being in the finest shopping mall in America.

Even without gambling you can be lucky. Look at this. On the bus they give each of us a lunch ticket which I can't use because I'm under a doctor's care for gallbladder. For me, this lunch ticket is deadly poison. I'll give it to you for two-fifty. It's a five-dollar value."

Winger says, "No, thanks."

Blitnis says, "I can't eat fresh food. Only canned or stale. A five-dollar value, Mr. Winger. You can have it for two dollars."

Winger says, "No thanks. I've got to be going." But he doesn't move because he notices this big guy, maybe six-five or six-six, who looks like he weighs three hundred pounds, wearing a light suit, standing nearby and looking him over. Then he realizes there are four more like him. One comes over to him and says, "Mr. Winger, would you come with us?"

Mrs. Blitnis is very surprised. She says, "Mr. Winger, how come you know these people? You must come here a lot."

The men in suits surround him and start to walk. Winger is in the middle and he's got no choice. Either he walks or they carry him along.

Mrs. Blitnis yells after them, "Mr. Winger! Be in touch! Maybe we'll come down on an excursion together."

They lead him to a little office. Another guy comes in and he says, "Mr. Winger, your bank in New York returned your check," and he shows him the check. It's stamped "Account Closed." The guy says, "This is a lot of money, Mr. Winger, and you gave us four more like it. What are you going to do about it?"

Winger says, "I'd like to talk to my lawyer."

The guy looks at him like he knows what's happening and he says, "If that's what you want that's the way we'll do it. We'll call the police. You can call your lawyer from the police station after you're booked."

Winger's heart is beating like crazy. He's never been inside a police station, let alone arrested. It's a very scary thing. He says, "I want to talk to my lawyer."

The guy calls the police. He knows all the cops by first name, like they're friends. In a few minutes Winger is in handcuffs and they take him down to this new jail and courthouse they got in Atlantic City and they book him.

12

I DON'T CLAIM TO KNOW ABOUT THE LAW OR THE police. What I know about cops I know from driving a cab. If a cop has not filled his ticket quota, he'll give you a ticket for nothing, for passing a yellow light, for not signaling, for making a left turn against a sign even if there's not another car in sight. You name it, he's there with the ticket—if he hasn't filled his quota. A ticket like that, a moving violation, costs me half a day's pay. I drive a twelve-hour shift. If I get a ticket, I'm driving six hours to pay for that ticket. That does not give me a warm feeling for cops. But if they already made their quota, it's a different story. If they made their quota you got nothing to worry about because then they don't give a damn what you do.

Winger's situation is not like getting a ticket. He's in jail. He's in jail for a gambling violation and down there gambling is religion. You get hauled in front of a judge for a gambling violation and they look at you like you're the scum of the earth.

I believe there's a reason for that. Atlantic City is one big gambling joint. Millions of dollars pass through those casinos every day. More money than anyone can imagine. When cash is flowing like that—no receipts, just cash going across the tables—everybody is going to want a piece of it. And who's dumb enough to say no to them? If you cut people in, they're your friend. I know what I'm willing to do for an extra buck. So with the amount of money they got down there they can get anybody to do anything, from top to bottom—fifty, a hundred, a thousand, something for everybody—and it won't add up to one day's intake. I got no proof that this is happening and I never heard that it's happening but I believe it is because it's human nature. It stands to reason. It's logical and it's good business. If everybody's covered, everybody's relying on the extra cash they get under the table and everybody's part of the action. If you come along and cheat a casino, you're messing with everybody's livelihood and everybody's mad at you.

Winger doesn't understand that. Maybe it would be worse for him if he did. I don't know how long he was in jail but finally they let him make a phone call and he calls this

Grenlily guy. Grenlily gets some local shyster to bail him out and a couple of hours later he's on a bus back to New York.

As soon as he gets back he's looking for me because I've got his key. He's also looking for Croppe. I'm a lot easier to find than Croppe is, so he finds me first. When he finds me it's Saturday afternoon and I'm in the Green Leaf. Winger comes in and the man looks bad. He looks scared, like somebody's after him. He sits down on the stool beside me at the bar and doesn't say anything. I say to Max, "Give this man a drink."

Winger says to me, "Do you have the key?"

I say, "I have it but not on me."

He says, "I don't know what I'm going to do."

I don't say anything because I don't know what's going on. All I knew was I got a key in an envelope postmarked Atlantic City. So I'm waiting for Winger to explain. If he wants sympathy he won't get it from me because he dragged me into something without asking my permission.

He's so nervous he can't sit still. He finishes his beer and says, "I've got to talk to you."

I say, "All right. Talk."

He says, "Let's go for a walk."

I say, "Which is it? You want to talk or you want to walk?"

But I can see the man needs help so I don't argue. I go out with him and we start walking on Roosevelt under the El. I don't like that. He's talking but I'm looking up at the tracks overhead. I've seen bolts fall off those tracks and I've heard stories about people getting hit on the head with them so I don't feel comfortable when I'm underneath. He starts telling me his story but I'm thinking about bolts so I cut him off. I say, "Listen, Dave, if you want to talk, let's go someplace and sit down and have a cup of coffee. I can't concentrate on what you're saying if I have to walk like this." So we go into a place and order coffee and pie. He starts at the beginning, with the blizzard, just the way I told it here. We were in this place for a long time and when he gets done he says to me, "What do I do? I have to get out of this."

I say, "What happened to Kathy Dellawood?"

He looks at me like I'm from another planet. He's not thinking of Kathy Dellawood. Then all of a sudden he says, "What's today?"

I tell him it's Saturday.

He says, "I have a date with her tonight. I've got to break it."

I say, "Why?"

He says, "I've got too much on my mind."

I say, "You got any money?"

He says, "I've got almost a thousand dollars. But I've got to pay it back to the bank. I've got to pay them fifty thousand dollars plus interest."

I say, "Listen to me. Go out with this girl. Blow some money on her. Show her a good time. Have some drinks, have dinner. You wake up in her bed Sunday morning and you'll feel a lot better. Believe me, that's what you need."

He says, "I've got to get out of this mess." Like he didn't hear a word I said.

I say, "I'll tell you the truth, Dave, I warned you. But you put yourself in that man's hands and he's got you. He's taking you for a ride. All you can do now is wait and see where he lets you out."

He says, "There's one thing I can do. I got forty-five thousand dollars in the bank in Atlantic City. I could pay all that back for starters. Then I'd only owe five thousand plus the interest."

I say, "Pay it back to who? The bank or the casino?"

He says, "I signed for it at the bank."

I say, "Either way, if you admit you got that money you're in trouble. They'll both want to collect—now you're talking about a hundred thousand—and it'll be evidence that you pulled a fraud in Atlantic City. You try to pay it back and you're going to be in worse trouble than you're in now."

He says, "What should I do?"

I said, "All you can do is wait and see what happens. You're in too deep to get out of it on your own. This is Croppe's scam. Your only chance is that Croppe is telling you the truth when he says you'll come out of it clean. So my advice, since you're so anxious for it, is don't do anything. Wait and see. That check the guy showed you was stamped 'Account Closed.' I've got to believe Croppe closed it and took the money. That means he's got fifty thousand out of this so far. He's got fifty and you got forty-five. He has to give the lawyer something. Maybe ten or twenty thousand to get you off. Maybe Croppe'll pay the lawyer out of that fifty thousand, give you five, six thousand to cover the bank with the interest, and still have twenty-five thousand for himself. You'd come out of it pretty clean then. If not, you're going to have to find yourself a lot of money. Don't ask me how. You're not going to make it painting. Just make sure that Croppe doesn't make you another offer that gets you into a worse mess. So all you can do now is wait and see. Get your mind off it the best way you can. Call up this Kathy Dellawood. That's my advice."

13

WELL, HE TOOK MY ADVICE AND THEN SOME. HE went crazy. I don't know what got into him. Maybe that week in Atlantic City turned his head. First he rented a white sports car. Then he gets dressed up in one of the outfits Croppe got him from Freddie and he goes over to Kathy Dellawood's place. She lives with a roommate somewhere in Sunny-side—two girls with a whole floor and two bedrooms. They drive to Manhattan, he pays maybe twenty dollars to park, picks up theater tickets, and they go to dinner. He spends big money on dinner and then they see the show. Champagne at intermission and after the show more drinks. Then he drives her home. She's very impressed with all this and she invites him in and just like I expected he wakes up Sunday morning in her bed.

But he's not happy. At least that's what he told me the next time I saw him. She's beautiful, she's impressed with him, but now that he got her into bed he doesn't like her. Why? Because the girl is only interested in money. But he knew that in the first place. He took Croppe's deal because of that. It just goes to show how confused he was in his own mind.

Sunday morning they're sitting in bed and he's telling her that money is not important. She agrees with him. She agrees with everything he says. She's no fool. She looks at it this way—she thinks the guy is rich, maybe a multimillionaire, because she doesn't know that the sports car is rented and that there's no more money for shows and dinners and champagne. She figures he's a little bit crazy—working as a painter and saying that money is not important—and that fits right in with her idea of how a rich guy should act. And she's right. Rich people grow up with nothing to worry about and that makes them crazy. So they manufacture trouble for themselves. You read about it in the paper all the time. And she figures that's what he's doing and she thinks it's terrific. Her mistake is that she's too hot for the money. She's got herself so convinced he's rich she practically dragged him into bed, which is not cool.

When I saw him again I asked him how it was with her. He doesn't want to talk about it. But I'm very curious. So I'm annoyed. Sometimes we'll sit for an hour and he'll give me every detail of his problems and even if I don't want to hear it, I'm polite and I listen. But when I want to know something, that's different. Then it occurs to me that maybe he did something stupid. So I said to him, "Did you tell her the truth? Did you tell her anything about Atlantic City?"

He says, "No. I wanted to but I didn't get around to it."

I said, "Take my advice and don't."

A couple of nights later Winger is up in his room and his doorbell rings. It's over a week since he got back from Atlantic City and he still hasn't been able to find Croppe. This is driving him nuts. They're leaving him high and dry with the law and the bank. But when the doorbell rings he's relieved. He figures it's Croppe and that means Croppe has not skipped out on him. He goes downstairs, all excited, opens the door—and there's Kathy Dellawood. A girl like that rings the bell of any normal man in the middle of the night and he has to think to himself that even though things are bad, this makes up for a lot of it. But not Winger. His face falls. She says to him, "What's wrong?" She's probably thinking he's got another girl upstairs.

He says, "Nothing's wrong. I'm glad to see you." But he's upset, and not just because he wanted it to be Al Croppe. He's upset because now she's going to see where he lives. He may say he's disappointed because she's only interested in money but, meanwhile, he doesn't want to do anything that will give her the impression he doesn't have it. I don't know what she thinks when she sees the place. She has to be a little crazy herself to believe a millionaire would live in a cheap furnished room like that with an old tan linoleum with blue flowers. But that just goes to show you how people talk themselves into things. Wishful thinking. She wants him to be rich and she's so hot for the money that she'll believe anything. But she says to him, "How come you live in a place like this?"

He figures this is the time to tell her the truth. But he doesn't. I asked him what he said to her. He says, "I don't remember."

I said, "What do you mean, you don't remember? You remember everything else, how come you don't remember that?"

He says, "Just some bullshit," which isn't even the way he talks. So I know he's embarrassed by what he said. He probably gave her a song and dance about wanting to know how his workers were going to live, or to get an idea of what it meant to earn the kind of salary he'd be paying. Whatever it was, it served the purpose and made her keep thinking he's rich. Pretty soon they're in bed, which is what they both want and why she's visiting him at ten o'clock at night in the first place.

Afterwards she's talking to him about business. She loves to talk about business. They're lying there talking and it's eleven, eleven-thirty at night and the doorbell rings again. His doorbell didn't ring for six months, now all of a sudden it rings twice in one night. Now he's really upset. He knows it's Croppe and he's got to talk to Croppe. But what's he going to do with this girl in his bed? He'd like to get rid of her because he's had his action on that front for the night and what he's got to talk to Croppe about is more important to him than this girl, but he can't just throw her out.

She says to him, "Who is it?"

He says, "It's probably business."

She says, "At this time of night?"

The bell rings again.

He gets up and starts to put on his pants. He says, "You better get dressed. I'll try to keep him downstairs but he may want to come up."

He goes down and the second he opens the door Croppe says to him, "Dave, Dave, am I glad to see you! We have to talk. A lot is happening."

Dave says, "I've been looking for you. I want to talk to you."

Al says, "We got problems. It's that shyster, Grenlily."

A little while ago Grenlily was a top lawyer—sharp, sharp, sharp. Now, all of a sudden, he's a shyster.

Croppe says, "He gave me bad advice. Let's go upstairs and I'll explain it to you."

Dave starts to ask him questions right there, downstairs in the hallway. Croppe says, "Wait. Let's go upstairs. I'll tell you the whole story upstairs." But Dave is stalling. He says, "What happened to the money? Why did the bank stamp 'Account Closed' on the check?"

Al says, "I'll explain that."

Dave says, "Go on. Explain it. What's the story?"

Al says, "What is it with you? You want to stand out here so everybody can hear us? Let's go upstairs."

Dave turns around and goes up the stairs very slow. He fiddles with the door like he can't get it open, just to give her more time to get dressed. Finally he opens the door and there's Kathy sitting in his bed, wearing his shirt with the top three or four buttons open and nothing else on. She's a fantastic sight but it's not what he expected to see. She didn't even try to get dressed. Winger doesn't understand anything. This situation is what she dreams about. She didn't want to get dressed. She thought this was the big stuff—a secret middle-of-the-night business talk, and there she is, a millionaire's mistress, in his bed, wearing his shirt, in his hideaway, and they're going to talk big money. This gets her hot. Power. Business. Secret meetings.

Croppe comes in, takes one look, and he's totally floored. This is not his idea of David Winger. This is totally unexpected. And that's bad news for Al because his scam depends on him knowing how Winger thinks. So Croppe has to reevaluate. He has to make sure Winger is not going to mess up his plans. But one thing about Al Croppe—he does not get rattled. I have to give him that. He does not so much as blink an eye. He takes off his hat—he's wearing his fur hat, fur coat, and maroon scarf—and he says, just like he was expecting to see her there, "Miss, I'm sorry to barge in on you at this ungodly hour of a winter night but David and I have business that couldn't wait till morning. The name is Croppe. Albert T. Croppe. C-r-o-p-p-e."

She says, "It's all right. Don't mind me. You go ahead and talk business. I'll be quiet as a mouse."

Croppe says, "Excuse me again, but I have to ask you a question. Who do you model for?"

She says, "What do you mean?"

He pulls out a business card and hands it to her. He says, "Do you have a portfolio?"

She says, "I don't know what you mean. I never modeled anything."

He says, "Does that mean you already have an agent and you're not interested in me?"

She says to Winger, "What's going on?"

Dave is mad. He says, "Don't believe him."

She shows him the card. It says "Albert T. Croppe. Modeling Agent."

Dave says, "Oh, no! He probably has all kinds of cards."

Croppe has this big friendly smile like he really likes them both. He says, "Dave, you're right. Listen to him, young lady. He knows. What he's saying to you is, 'Don't get into modeling.' It has ruined more nice girls than anything else. You know why? I'll tell you what happens. A girl like you is spotted and as soon as her portfolio gets around she finds herself on magazine covers. Just like that. Famous overnight. I know this business and I know what they're looking for. You'll be in ads, posters, everywhere. Everybody will want you. Before you know it you'll have the movie people offering you contracts. It happens so fast it takes your breath away. I've seen it. And you are the one it will happen to because you have what they want. All this probably sounds very glamorous. You're rich overnight, you're dating celebrities, royalty, but, believe me, I speak from experience, I have a list of successful models under contract to me and I've seen this happen—that kind of sudden wealth and fame is the most destructive thing you can imagine. I have seen more nice, sweet girls, like yourself, spoiled by it than by anything else. What Dave is saying is that he doesn't want that to happen to you."

Dave says, "Don't listen to him. He's not a modeling agent."

Al says, "That's right. Stick to your guns, Dave. And Miss—I didn't get your name—"

She says, "Katherine Dellawood."

He says, "Miss Dellawood, he's doing you a favor. Remember, I'm telling you myself. If you were to call the number on that card you might come to regret it. All those stories about big stars alone in their Hollywood castles are true. You could end up like that. Marilyn Monroe. Gloria Swanson. It's not a happy life. So don't let me lead you astray. Because I, personally, as a professional, would not talk you out of it. For me, having someone with your potential under contract is too great a temptation to pass up. I've been in this business a long time but I've never been struck so quickly— you, on the bed—the minute I walked in, you must have noticed my reaction, Miss Dellawood. The second I crossed the threshold I said to myself, This is the girl. You heard the expression, 'Her face is her fortune'? That's you. Do you read poetry? I'm a big fan of poetry. To me, it expresses the heart. When I need to say something from the heart I find that Shakespeare said it best. He said, 'Where your treasure is, there your heart is.' Keep it in mind. You're a wonderful girl, don't let your beauty ruin you. Now, if you'll forgive my intrusion on this cold winter night, Dave and I have business to talk about."

She says, "Please, don't apologize. You're very flattering. I'd like to talk to you when you have time."

Al says, "Thank you very much. My voice may sound emotional right now but it's because I'm holding myself back from telling you that you have only to sign a contract and your career is made. I won't do that. Stick with Dave here. Do what he tells you. Now, Dave, let's talk about our little problem. You know that once in a while a business gets a sudden cash drain. When that happens if you don't come up with the cash you have to sell something or borrow. I don't have to tell you that. You must understand that your-self, Miss Dellawood. It just so happens that in one of my ventures I was squeezed for cash last week. I needed fifty thousand dollars cash immediately. When you get in that position, the first thing you do, as you know, is you see your lawyer. So I went to Donnie Grenlily and told him the story. He said to me, 'If you need cash, if you need it in dollar bills right away, it's too late for a bank loan.' He said, 'You can't arrange a sale in that time either. Not for cash. So why don't you just take the fifty thousand you've got available to you.' I didn't know what he was talking about. I said, 'Donnie, what fifty thousand? I don't have any such thing.' He says, 'Yes you do. You got it in Dave Winger's account.'"

Al says, "Believe me, when I heard that I was shocked. I know Donnie Grenlily a long time and I never thought he'd give me a piece of advice like that. I said, 'Donnie, how can you think of such a thing? That boy's down in Atlantic City giving checks on that account. If I take the money out, those checks will bounce and that boy is in big trouble.' Now, to show you what lawyers are like in this day and age, he says to me, 'He's not in trouble. That's the beauty of the system I gave you for cashing those checks. If he did it just like I told you, nobody can say he cashed those checks. What do you think that whole setup was about?'

"This made my head spin. The man is such a conniver."

I'm a little surprised that Al Croppe talked like that in front of the girl. She's a stranger. She could go down to the hotel and give away the whole thing and become a second witness against Winger, which, from what Croppe says, is all the hotel needs. But maybe that's not the way things are done. I don't know. Or maybe he already smelled her out and that's what the whole modeling contract talk was about. The man has an instinct for people.

Al says to Dave, "I know what you're thinking and I agree with you. I don't like it either. I cursed him out. I said, 'You mean you set me up for this? Me and this boy?' He says, 'I didn't set you up. I did just the opposite. I gave you a system that protects you. You can take this money out of the bank and still be okay.' "

Al says, "I was in a real bind. I was squeezed. When people get you like that there is no mercy. I stood to lose a lot of money. I won't say how much but, believe me, when I say a lot I mean a lot. So I had no choice. I didn't like it but I did it. I saved the business and I thought, Well, I'm sorry it had to be this way but at least it's over with. But what I didn't know was that I was being naive because that's just where the problem started. Today Donnie calls me up and says, 'How much have you got in that safe deposit box?' I said, 'I personally have got nothing in there.' He says, 'Never mind

the games. How much is in the safe deposit box?' I say, 'I
don't know and I don't have the key. It's not mine and I can't
get it and I wouldn't get it if I could.' But he insists so I had
to tell him, 'I think it's forty-five thousand.' He says, 'That's
good because that happens to be my fee.' I say, 'Donnie, do
you know what you're saying? You're leaving that boy with
a bank bill of fifty thousand dollars plus interest. It was bad
enough before but now you're completely ruining him.' He
says, 'Did the hotel have him arrested?' I say, 'Yes.' He says,
'When they go to court are they going to have any evidence?' I say, 'No.' He says, 'Then it's a false arrest. They are
liable for that. We will sue them and collect a quarter of a
million dollars. That boy will pay off the bank and be sitting
pretty with two hundred thousand in his pants.' I say, 'Donnie, I don't know. I'll talk to him but he may not go for it.
He's a guy who will spend his whole life working off that
debt before he'd get rich that way.' He says, 'Nobody's such
an idiot.' I'm just telling you what he said. He says, 'Nobody's such an idiot. Go talk to him.' So that's why I'm here.
That's the story. Now it's up to you. You got the trial soon.
Donnie tells me the outcome is sure. He'll show them your
handwriting on your ID; they'll look at the handwriting on
the checks; they're completely different; and it's all over. So
he'll get you off but he wants all the money in the safe
deposit box. You got to decide what's the next step. You got
to pay the bank. You sue the hotel and you'll come out of it
clean and you'll be rich. A quarter of a million dollars. But
this is all up to you. I can't help you. Just tell me what you
want to do, Dave.''

14

DRIVING OLD PEOPLE TO THE DOCTOR'S IS A BIG
part of the business in any Queens car service. The next morning, after Al visited
Dave and saw Kathy in his bed, that's what
I happened to be doing. I was driving an old
couple to the doctor's. At that time I didn't
know what happened in Dave's apartment
the night before. Now since I say that,
maybe I ought to explain something else.
I'm telling this story in the order it happened, not in the order I found out about it.
I got a piece of it here, a piece of it there,
from different people, and it was a long time
before I had the whole thing. But it would

not make sense to tell it that way, so I'm telling it the way it actually happened, although at the time it was happening I didn't know what was actually happening—if you follow me. And while I'm straightening that out, let me mention something else. You might have noticed that when I was talking about taking people to the doctor's I said car service when before this I was saying cab. Somebody explained to me that when I say cab I confuse people. I don't actually drive a cab. A cab has a meter and people stand on the street and wave it down. I drive for a car service. I don't have a meter and I don't stop for people waving at me on the street. The way you get a car service is you call on the phone and tell the dispatcher where you want to go and where to pick you up. In a cab you pay by the meter and they charge for time and mileage. With me, they give you a flat rate over the phone according to the distance and the price stays the same no matter how long it takes or what route I go by.

On this day I got a call to go to an address on Ketchem Street. I pick up the old couple on Ketchem and they're going to a doctor on Dry Harbor Road. I head down Broadway to Queens Boulevard and as we're passing the Georgia Diner and Macy's, which are across the street on the side going to Manhattan, the old lady points to the diner and says to the old man, "That's where we get it." She says to me, "If I want to get the bus to Atlantic City at eight o'clock tomorrow morning, what time do I have to call for a car?"

I say, "You can call any time. You can call right now. Just tell them to be there by quarter to eight. But don't call later than seven-fifteen in the morning, maybe even seven o'clock, because it's busy then."

She says, "We're going to Atlantic City. Last time I was a big winner."

He says, "Some winner!"

She says, "I was ahead ninety-eight dollars and I was ready to go home but when you go by bus you got to leave when the bus wants to leave, not when you want to. While I was waiting for the bus I lost the whole ninety-eight dollars."

He says, "This kind of thing is psychological. The gambler is gambling from psychological necessity. That's why she's never satisfied with what she wins. So she keeps playing till she loses. Then she's really not satisfied. It's like the dog and the manager. The dog doesn't eat the hay and neither does the manager so nobody gets it. When I go to Atlantic City I don't gamble. I study the psychology."

She says, "You think we'll see Mr. Winger again? I hate to see a young man like that lose his shirt. Who would have guessed him for a gambler?"

The old guy says, "It's not from gambling he'll lose his shirt. It's those fellows who came for him. He better not hang around with them."

She says, "I'm going to call him up and talk to him."

He says, "Why is that your responsibility? And, besides, he doesn't have a phone."

She says, "A nice young man and he's going to get in trouble."

They go on like that and I'm listening and wondering if I

should tell them I know Winger. It's a chancy business. It might seem like you'd get a bigger tip if you had a mutual acquaintance. But not necessarily. Sometimes people take you for a friend and you don't tip a friend. Sometimes they're afraid you overheard something they don't want you to. So you could wind up with nothing. Who knows what happened between Winger and these people? Maybe I don't want to get involved. My motto is, the less said the better. So I listen and say nothing and I don't hear anything I don't already know.

That night I get a phone call from Dave Winger. He's at the Green Leaf and he tells me he wants the key. I can tell from his voice that he's upset.

I get my coat and tell Brenda I'm going for a walk. She gives me a look because she knows I don't go out late at night. Not when I got to get up at five in the morning. And not when it's that cold outside. She says to me, "Is anything wrong?"

I say, "No."

She says, "How about we take a walk together? I'd like to get out too."

I say, "Not tonight."

When I get to the Green Leaf Dave is standing by the door. As soon as he sees me, before he says hello or anything else, he says, "Do you have the key?"

I say, "Sure."

He says, "Good. Let me have it."

I say, "Let's go dig it up."

He says, "What do you mean—'Dig it up'?"

I say, "I buried it."

He looks at me like I'm crazy. He says, "Are you serious?"

I say, "Yes, I'm serious. Why?"

He says, "I don't believe you."

I say, "So don't believe me."

He says, "You buried it? Russ! Did you put it in anything? Did you just stick it in the ground? How are we going to find it?"

I don't think it's such a bad idea and I don't like that he gets so upset. What did he expect me to do with it? Wear it around my neck? I didn't ask him for the key. If he doesn't like what I do he should have mailed it to somebody else.

I lead him over to 30th Avenue where it dead-ends up against the Brooklyn-Queens Expressway. There's what you might call a park there, but it's more like an empty lot. It's a cold night, the wind is blowing, the place is full of junk, and it's still got a lot of ice and snow. There's probably rats in there too. I stop and look around. I'm thinking. He hasn't told me about Al Croppe visiting him last night and saying that his lawyer wants the whole forty-five thousand, so I don't know about that yet. All I know is that the money's down there in Atlantic City, big piles of it in a box which I'm holding the key for.

He's looking at the lot and he says, "In here?"

I'm looking at the lot too. I say, "Somewhere in here."

He says, "What do you mean, 'somewhere'?"

I say, "We got to look."

He says, "For God's sake, Russ! What the hell is wrong with you? Don't you know where it is?"

I say, "Nothing is wrong with me, Dave."

He says, "What kind of thing is it to bury a key? We'll never find it in here."

I say, "Did you ever hear of Captain Kidd?"

He says, "What the hell are you talking about?"

I say, "What do you think Captain Kidd did with his treasure? Captain Kidd. Bluebeard. They all buried the stuff. It's the only safe way to hide anything."

He says, "If I didn't know you better I'd think you were trying to put something over on me."

I said to him, "Who asked you to send me the key? And what makes you think I got a better place to put it? Do I have a safe place in my apartment? Do I have a lot of room? Do I have privacy, for God's sakes? I got two kids and a wife in two little bedrooms. We're on top of each other. If my wife finds a safe deposit box key won't she ask me what it is? What do you think she'll say if I tell her I got the key to a box where somebody's hiding forty-five thousand dollars he got in a scam in Atlantic City? She's gonna say, 'What kind of an idiot are you to hold a key like that and get nothing out of it?' That's what she'll say. So I had to hide it someplace where she wouldn't see it. You sent it to me and I hid it—no complaints, no questions. I came out on a cold night and buried the fucking thing and now you're complaining because I can't find it! I don't need this, Dave. I didn't ask for it and I don't need it."

He says, "Okay, okay. Let's look."

We start to look. The whole situation is very unpleasant. It's cold, there's broken glass, and this is the kind of place where people go to piss in the bushes. We're looking for maybe ten, twenty minutes but it seems like hours. Finally I say, "Maybe we should come back during the daytime."

He says, "Did you bury it during the day?"

I say, "No."

He says, "Then you're more likely to recognize the place at night. It won't look as familiar during the day. Do you think anybody saw you bury it?"

I say, "That's why I did it at night."

So we keep looking. He keeps asking, "Do you remember this rock? How about this bush? Or this bump? Or this pile of junk?" I'm never sure. I must have sounded like an idiot. We keep looking and looking and he keeps saying, "I can't believe this! I can't believe this!"

After a while he tells me what happened last night with Kathy and Al in his room. It comes out that he needs the forty-five thousand to stay out of jail. At that point I start to feel guilty. He doesn't tell me yet that he could sue for a quarter of a million.

The wind is blowing. The place is freezing. It's so cold that I've got tears in my eyes. Finally he says, "Let's leave it for tonight."

I say, "What are you going to do?"

He doesn't answer.

We walk back toward Roosevelt and I start trying to make him feel better. I say, "I'll come back tomorrow by myself and I'm sure I'll recognize the place and I'll find it." But he doesn't say a word. At Broadway we split. He goes his way and I go mine.

When I walked over to the Green Leaf that night to meet him I had no plan. I had no intention. I wasn't thinking of telling him anything but the truth. But when he asked me I just said, "I buried it," without thinking. I don't know why. I had the key in my pocket. I was holding it in my hand. I meant to give it to him. But it was forty-five thousand dollars. I just wasn't prepared in my mind to let it go so fast. But I wasn't going to steal it or keep it from him.

He used me without asking my permission and he didn't even appreciate that I was taking a risk for him for no reward. But I didn't want the key. I figured I'd give him the key the next day. I'd just tell him I remembered where it was and went back and dug it up.

15

THE NEXT DAY, AFTER MY SHIFT, I DROPPED IN AT the Green Leaf looking for him. I asked Max for a beer and I said to him, "Have you seen Dave Winger?"

He looks around, nods, and very quiet says, "He went to Atlantic City this afternoon. Rented a car."

I nod and act like it's no big deal but he stands there looking at me. I thought maybe Dave told him about the key and Max is too smart to believe I buried it so he's going to ask me where the key is and what I think I'm doing. He looks around a little more and then he says to me in a very quiet voice,

"Don't say I told you but Al Croppe and Sid General went down there after him in Sid's car."

I have one beer and get out of there. That whole night I can't sleep. The alarm goes off at 5 A.M. and it's still dark when I go to work. I sign out a car, get gas, and when I come out of the gas station I radio in that I'm ready. I get a call to Jackson Heights. A stewardess going to LaGuardia. You get this a lot at 6 A.M. Stewardesses on early-morning flights. They don't have fancy addresses either. I used to think stewardess was a glamour job and I expected them to live in fancy places and give wild parties but the ones I pick up live in two-, three-family brick houses which are nothing special, although I wouldn't mind if I could afford one. They're not big tippers either.

I drop her off and come out of LaGuardia but I don't call in like I'm supposed to. I head down 94th Street and before it turns into Junction Boulevard I cut back to Jackson Heights and go to Dave Winger's address. I get out of the car without radioing in what I'm doing and ring his bell. I got the key in my pocket. It's 6:30 in the morning, maybe a little later. I wait. No answer. I ring again. Nothing. I can't stand there for long because they may try to call me on the radio. I press the buzzer and hold it in. If he got back from Atlantic City very late last night he may be sound asleep. But he doesn't answer so I have to think that maybe he didn't get back at all. This makes me worry about Al and Sid following him down there. Who knows what happened?

A guy in a T-shirt with a beer belly comes to the door. He says to me, "Whadda ya want?"

I say, "I'm looking for Dave Winger."

He says, "He ain't in."

I say, "Did he go out this morning?"

He says, "He never came back last night."

I say, "Who are you?"

He says, "I'm the landlord."

I say, "Are you sure?"

He says, "Whatta you mean, 'Am I sure'? I gotta show you the deed? Who are you?"

I say, "I mean, are you sure he never came back."

He says, "You wanna go up and knock? Go up and knock."

I go up and knock. "Dave! Dave!" I say. Nothing.

I go down to the street and get into my car. I start the engine, the radio comes on, and right away I hear, "Car number one-forty-four, Russ, car number one-forty-four, Russ, where are you?"

I radio back, "Car number one-forty-four. I'm just coming out of LaGuardia."

He bawls me out for not answering the radio before. "Pay attention to the radio," he says. Then he gives me an address and tells me to get there fast. The place is up on Astoria Boulevard, near LaGuardia, which is where they think I am, so I start heading there. I pass a phone booth on a street corner and I put on the brakes, pull over, and get out. I ask information for Kathy Dellawood in Sunnyside. Luckily there's only one K. Dellawood in Sunnyside and the operator gives me the number. I call and get this sleepy girl's voice. I say, "Kathy?"

The girl is yawning. She says, "Who is this?"

I say, "You don't know me. I'm a friend of Dave Winger. I got to get in touch with him. It's an emergency."

She says, "He went to Atlantic City."

I say, "I know that but do you know where he went in Atlantic City or when he was planning to come back?"

She says, "Who is this?"

I say, "My name is Russ. You don't know me but Dave has told me a lot about you."

She says, "This isn't Kathy. Kathy went with Dave."

It takes me a second to straighten that out in my head, then I say to her, "Do you know where in Atlantic City they went?"

She says, "How do I know you're really a friend of his?"

I say, "Why else would I call and ask all these questions early in the morning. I was at his place and he wasn't there."

She says, "What's the deal with him? Is he rich and just fooling around as a painter or what? I don't like what's going on there."

I say, "The guy is loaded. He's a playboy. You know the deal."

She says, "Where does he get his money?"

I say, "From his parents."

She says, "I know that but where do they get it from?"

I say, "From business."

She gets annoyed. She says, "I know that. But what business are they in? Oil? Stocks? Real estate? What is it?"

I say, "It's family money. His father is in some kind of family business."

She says, "Why don't you give me a straight answer?"

I say, "I'm telling you what I know."

She says, "This doesn't smell right to me. Kathy's my friend and I'm not going to stand by and see her hurt."

I say, "Look, I'll be glad to call you back and give you any details you want but right now I got an emergency call from his bank and I got to get in touch with him."

She says, "It's seven o'clock in the morning. The banks aren't open yet."

I say, "It's his bank in Tokyo."

She says, "I don't like this. I don't like it at all."

I say, "Listen, miss, I got an emergency here. Tokyo is on the line and they want an answer. Where in Atlantic City is Dave Winger?"

She says, "Are you calling from a phone booth? I hear street noises."

I say, "I'm on a street in Ohio. I just got the call from Tokyo and my office isn't open yet. I'm on my way to work. I stopped off at a phone booth."

She says, "I don't trust you."

What can I say? The girl already must think I'm an idiot. I give up and it's quiet on the line for a few seconds and then she says, "I'll tell you what I know but I don't like it. All I know is he called her yesterday and asked if she wanted to go to Atlantic City. They rented a car and went down there. From the way she was talking it sounds like something fishy is going on."

I say, "Thank you for the information." That was a lot of trouble for nothing.

I drive the car back to the garage and radio the dispatcher. I say, "Car number one-forty-four. I'm just outside. I can't take that call. I got a family emergency. I need a ride to the Georgia Diner."

The dispatcher says, "What kind of emergency you got at the Georgia Diner?"

I say, "It's a family emergency."

He gives me a hard time. He wants to know how did I hear about it because nobody called in and I didn't say anything about getting off the seat to make a call myself. I give him a hard time right back. I don't care. They're not going to fire me. Good drivers are hard to find. Who wants to work for this kind of money? Maybe if they fired me I'd be better off. I'd go out and get a better job. I turn in the money I got for the ride to LaGuardia, except my share of it, which, with what I got in my pocket, gives me maybe twenty-five dollars. I get a ride to the Georgia, pay the driver, and tip him. No free rides from this company.

There's a little crowd waiting for the bus and I see the old couple I drove to the doctor's the day before yesterday. They don't recognize me but I see them look at me and then talk to each other like I look familiar but they can't figure out who I am. The woman is carrying a big bag with lunch or breakfast, probably both. She's already giving the guy an apple. He's got a book. The bus comes and by eight o'clock I'm on my way to Atlantic City.

Five minutes later we hit the Brooklyn-Queens Expressway and I'm already figuring this has to be the stupidest thing I ever did in my life. First of all, how am I going to find

him? Second of all, he may be on his way back already.
Third of all, I don't know what's going on. Maybe he just
took off on a lark with his girlfriend. And, if not, if it's a bad
situation like I'm thinking of, how am I going to rescue him
from Al Croppe and Sid General? If I find them I'm going to
get caught in the middle. And I don't even know what this is
really all about. The best thing for me to do is what I always
do—keep out of it. But here I am, heading for Atlantic City
with my guilty conscience. If I just gave him the key instead
of telling him about Bluebeard the Pirate I'd be driving my
cab right now. It's the stupidest thing I can imagine.

We're out on the Gowanus Expressway and pretty soon I
see the Verrazano Bridge. At least the ride won't cost me
anything. They give you a voucher for lunch and they give
you back what they charge for the ride because they figure
everybody's going to lose it right back anyway. But I'm
going to keep the money, have the free lunch, and come out
ahead.

I try to sleep but I can't. I hear that old couple arguing.
She's telling him she never loses at blackjack.

It's a long trip and it seems like all these people know each
other, like it's a social club. We're cruising down the Garden
State Parkway when for no reason I can see, this woman
from the day before yesterday gets up and comes back to
where I'm sitting. She says to me, "I know you from someplace."

I shake my head.

She says, "Don't I look familiar to you?"

I say, "No. I see a lot of faces and I got a bad memory for faces."

All of a sudden she yells, "You're the cabdriver! That's it! From the other day! Harry! It's the cabdriver! What's your name?"

"Russ," I say.

She says, "Russ, are you going to Atlantic City?"

Where else does she think the bus is going?

She says, "Don't make it a habit. You can lose your shirt in Atlantic City. Let me tell you some of the ropes. The first thing, lesson number one, stay away from slots and roulette. Crap maybe. But best is blackjack."

I say, "I don't plan to gamble."

She says, "Plan is one thing. Do is another. But if you don't want to gamble talk to my husband. Harry! I got a teetotaler here."

He turns around and says to me, "Good for you. I don't gamble either. There's plenty to do in Atlantic City without gambling."

He gets up, comes back to where I am, and sits next to me. The next thing I know, he starts lecturing me. He's talking into my ear like it's a hole and he's trying to fill it up. He won't leave me alone. He shows me his book, *The Carnegie Report on Education in America.* I don't even understand what the title means, for God's sakes, and he's lecturing me on that book and everything else. I can't get away from him. We're on a bus. Where can I go? It's like a cage.

I was stuck with him the whole way and he never stopped

talking. When I shut my eyes he said, "Are you listening?" I said, "I'm just resting my eyes."

But it's a funny thing. A guy sits there talking nonsense and you're not listening but something he says hits you and starts you thinking about something else entirely—if you follow what I mean.

Brenda tells me I should have more ambition. She tells me how smart I am and that I could be a success if I got a better job or went into business. I'll say this for Brenda. She respects me. And she's right. I should get out and do something different. But I don't like to be tied down. I don't like driving a cab but at least I'm out in the open. I'm on the streets. I'm getting around. I'm not tied to a desk or a store. But Brenda is right. I don't look ahead. I never say, "I'll do this for ten years," or, "In twenty years I'll be doing that." I take it one day at a time and that's no good. If you do that for your whole life, all of a sudden, one day, you wake up and it's gone, ten, twenty, fifty years and you're still driving a cab. I can see myself thirty years from now, when I'm seventy-five years old—if I should live that long—I'll still be driving a cab. I've got no retirement money. I'll drop dead behind the wheel and that'll be the end of it. My whole life. I'll have white hair and some young guy who's a little kid today will be the dispatcher and he'll yell at me, "Pay attention to the radio!"

I'm sitting there in the bus thinking of this and meanwhile the guy says to me, "Aristotle spoke from cards."

I wasn't listening to him and I don't know if that was part

of something else he was talking about or what. I only noticed he said that because I heard it before. I said to him, "Somebody else told me that. What does it mean?"

He says, "Lecture cards. The man was a lecturer. They have all the cards he used for his lectures preserved in the Library of Paris in France. That's how they know what he said. They make books out of those lectures."

I say, "How do you know that?"

He says, "I was in the grocery business for thirty-seven years. I speak seven languages. We had customers from all over the world. Rich and poor. Every nationality. That's an education in itself. When I retired I started to read books. People today don't read books. They watch television. On television everything has to be excitement—pictures, action, fighting. Everything is blown out of context. As a consequence people are ignorant. To me, ignorance is the biggest problem in the world today. Ignorance is hanging over the whole world like the Sword of Damascus."

He says that this book which he's got on his lap has a theory of education which is full of ignorance. He says, "With education the story is like the golden goose eggs. You try to get the golden goose eggs before they're ready and you kill the golden goose. Education today is the same thing. Children finish school too soon. They should go to school all year long until they're twenty-five years of age. That's the only way you build up an educated population."

I say, "If I had to support my kids until they're twenty-five, I'd starve to death."

He says, "Let the government do it."

I say, "That's a good idea. Let the government do it right now. Why wait till they're twenty-five?"

And we're talking like that the whole way. Anything that comes up, he's got an answer. But he wasn't so bad. It passed the time. Otherwise it's a four-hour ride.

16

FINALLY WE GET TO ATLANTIC CITY AND THE BUS
drops us at a casino. Now the question is
how to find Winger. I go to the cashier to
trade in my voucher. They won't give me
bills. Chips or coins. I take rolls of quarters
and go to the casino so in case they're
watching it'll look like I'm here to gamble.
But I keep going through the casino, down
the corridor to the hotel. The safe deposit
box key is still in my pocket and it's got the
name of a bank on it. I ask the hotel cashier
how to get to this bank. He tells me the
nearest branch is on Pacific Street, which is
the first street in from the boardwalk. The

bank is a couple of blocks up Pacific from the street this hotel is on. I head for Pacific and then up Pacific to the bank. What I'm going to do when I get there I haven't figured out.

I get to the corner where the bank is and I'm about to cross the street when I notice this gray limousine with New York plates parked there. Limousines with New York plates are not rare in Atlantic City, so even though it's a shock I don't exactly drop dead. It could be anybody. But I did something stupid. I stood there trying to see who's inside. By the time I realized that it was Al Croppe, he's looking at me. Now I *am* ready to drop dead. I turn around and head back down Pacific as fast as I can go. I go one block and cut in to a street going toward the boardwalk. Sitting behind the wheel of a car all day does not put me in the best of shape so I'm already out of breath. I get to a hotel—all the hotels and casinos are on the boardwalk—and I look back. I don't see them coming so either they didn't see me and they're not chasing me or they're chasing me and they're about to come around that corner. Sid is fat so he has to be pretty slow and Croppe is probably in worse shape than I am. I know he drinks. Every time he has a cup of coffee there's a shot of booze in it. I'm out of breath but I have to believe I can move faster than they can. I don't wait to find out. I go into the hotel, through the casino, out to the boardwalk, and keep going. There's the Atlantic Ocean, right out there on my left but I don't have time to appreciate the sights. I go block after block, pass one casino, another, another, and finally I duck into one which has a row of white plaster statues of men wearing sheets and sandals like in the Roman Empire. I go through a revolving door and I'm inside.

It's not dark in there but it's not bright either. It's not crowded but it's not empty. It's not how I'd choose it but it's good enough so I can hide. I go to a section where they have slot machines and I take a machine way in the back, against the wall. If they come in here I'll see them before they see me. There's a lot of doors and I'm close enough to one of them so I can slip out. I take out a roll of quarters. I know that if I tear it open and let them all out I'll blow the whole thing. I peel back a little bit of paper so I can take out one quarter at a time. I put in the first one, pull the handle, and all of a sudden bells go off, lights start to blink, and the handle jams. The bells ring and ring and I'm dying. They're so loud that everybody's looking around to see who it is. I can't believe this. I'm the most conspicuous person in Atlantic City. They let them ring a long time because they want people to hear it. Finally a woman in a red and white striped suit comes over and says, "Congratulations! You hit the jackpot!"

I say, "How much?"

She says, "One thousand dollars!"

I say, "I don't believe it!"

She says, "It's true," and she turns off the bells and they give me a certificate for a thousand dollars and say, "Just take this to the cashier."

For once in my life, finally, I win something. But I can't stop to enjoy it because I got two guys chasing me. I go to the cashier and she says, "Would you like that in chips?" I say, "No, give me big bills." She looks at me like I'm a cheapskate or something, like I'm a bad sport, like I'm the kind of guy who quits when he's winning. But I don't care. This is no Wednesday night poker game with the boys. She starts to count, "One hundred, two hundred, three hundred, four hundred . . . ," and I'm looking around to see if they're after me. Everything looks normal but they could come through a door any second. I should be watching her count but I can't concentrate. I'm really discombobulated. She's counting and counting. This is a lot of money. I take out my wallet which, let me tell you, is skinny. This is a starving wallet. If I put those ten bills in my wallet it'll split the seams. So I roll them up and shove them in my pocket. Now I got three rolls of quarters on one side and a roll of ten hundred-dollar bills on the other. I feel like my pants are going to fall down. If I have to run now, I can't do it. I turn around and, believe me, at that point I forgot why I was there. All I wanted was to get back to New York with that thousand dollars. I could see myself laying five hundred dollars on the kitchen table and saying to Brenda, "Pay the grocery bill, pay the telephone bill, pay the electric bill, then take the rest and buy yourself some clothes." And I'll still have five hundred for myself. The problem is the bus doesn't leave until six o'clock. I've got to get through five more hours and there's nothing around here but gambling—slot machines, roulette, black-jack, craps, you name it. I don't even want to think about it. You see all that money and a thousand dollars is nothing. If I won a couple of bets in craps or roulette I could take home an even bigger pile. The only way to survive that temptation is to stay away from the casinos. But I also got Croppe and Sid General to worry about.

I got the five-dollar lunch voucher but it's only good at the hotel where the bus dropped us off. I go out to the board-walk and look around. The coast is clear. I'm walking back to the hotel and I'm like a madman. I'm laughing to myself. I got one hand in my pocket holding a thousand dollars, the other hand holding three rolls of quarters to keep them from bouncing. My eyes are popping out of my head and my head is going back and forth like a radar because I'm looking everywhere in case I see Croppe or Sid General. I get to the hotel. I buy a paper and I look for a place to eat. I find a cheap place, get a table, sit down, order lunch, and put the paper up in front of my face. I have no idea what I'm reading. All of a sudden I hear, "Russ, what are you doing here?" and I nearly drop dead. For a couple of beats my heart pumped so hard that I thought it damaged itself. I knew it wasn't Al Croppe. A second later I knew it was Dave Winger. I was scared anyway. I was so confused by running into Croppe, winning that thousand dollars, and everything else that I didn't know what I was doing or who I was hiding from or why I was hiding. I even forgot I came down there looking for Dave. I thought I was hiding from him too and when he said hello I felt like I was caught.

He says, "I saw you and I knew it was you but I didn't believe it. What are you doing here?"

I say, "I'm looking for you."

He says, "For me? How'd you know where I was?"

I say, "I found the key." I reach into my pocket to get the key but all I feel is that fat wad of hundreds. I know the key is in there but I can't take out the wad because I don't want anybody to know I have the money. We're talking and while we're talking I'm working around and around my pocket to get the key.

He's saying, "But I don't understand how you knew I was here."

I say, "I called your girlfriend and her roommate told me. I didn't know you'd be in this restaurant. As a matter of fact, when I was on the bus coming down here I was thinking it was a golden goose chase but I figured you really needed the key so it's worth taking a chance."

He says, "You took a day off from work?"

I say, "Anything for a friend." I was kidding but at the same time I wanted him to appreciate that I made a sacrifice for him. But I don't think he did appreciate it. He looked like he doubted me. I got the key out of my pocket and handed it to him.

He says, "Where did you find it?"

I say, "Right where I buried it."

He's looking at the key, feeling it, like it's missing something. He says, "So you did bury it."

I say, "I told you I buried it. Did you think I was lying?"

He says, "Did you put it in something or did you just stick it in the ground like this?"

I say, "It was in a little cardboard box."

He says, "Maybe that's why it didn't get rusty. But the cardboard must have rotted. Did it rot?"

I say, "What kind of test is this? Either you believe me or you don't. If you don't believe me, just say so."

He says, "You're a real character, Russ." And he's still feeling up the key. He says, "Come on over and meet Kathy."

I look over to where he's pointing and there she is. She's looking at us. And she is beautiful. Just like he said. Just like Croppe said. You'd think she's an actress. I go over to the table with him and we sit down. He introduces me but I don't like the way he does it. He says, "This is Russ. You remember I told you about Russ. The guy who thinks he's Captain Kidd."

She laughs.

I'm insulted and I'm very annoyed at Dave. Part of the reason I'm so mad, besides just that he's belittling me, is that this girl is so beautiful I want to make a good impression on her. I realize she's a twenty-three-, twenty-four-year-old girl, she's his girlfriend, she's a college graduate who is not in any way, shape, or form interested in me and never will be—and I'm not even dreaming of there being anything between us—but I want to make a good impression on her because she's so beautiful. I want her to like me. It's stupid and I know it but that's the way it is. Sometimes I think I don't care how Brenda feels about me. Brenda is not beautiful. But if you ask me, she's worth ten of this girl. I know that and even so I don't worry about Brenda but I want to make a good impression on this girl. But he introduces me in a way that makes me sound ridiculous. I feel like they're laughing at me. He tells her I found the key and she gets this funny smile. She says, "Then we can go right over and take out the money."

He says, "Let's finish lunch first." But I feel like something's wrong with the way they're talking. It annoys me so I decide to throw a little chill into them.

I say, "I don't know if this will have any effect on your plans but Al Croppe and Sid General are parked out in front of the bank in Sid's limousine."

She says, "When did you see them?"

I say, "About an hour ago. I think they saw me too."

They look at each other again. They don't say anything. The waiter brings my lunch and takes away their plates. They order dessert. Nobody's talking but I see them looking at each other. I start to eat. I'm eating and thinking and nobody's talking. All of a sudden I realize what's going on. I have the key. I told him I can't find the key. Then I come to Atlantic City with the key. I go to the bank where the money is—which I told them without realizing it when I said that Al and Sid were at the bank. I don't go in the bank because Al and Sid are out front. Then I come here and run into them without meaning to. What does that add up to? They believe I came to steal the money. He was suspicious as soon as I told him about burying the key and she must have given him an earful about that story. I don't know how smart she is but I think I've got her pegged. I know how greedy she is. Once they believe I lied about the key, even though I gave him the key, they're still suspicious of me. But I can't say anything because I don't want them to know that such things even occur to me. All I can do is act like nothing's wrong. They're having dessert but I don't feel like dessert. I'm already over the five dollars on the voucher.

The girl says, "If the three of us go over there together that might make too many people for them to try to bother us."

Dave says, "Three's not enough."

I say, "If you need people I can get two more."

He says, "Who?"

I say, "You remember that old couple, the Blitnises? You did their apartment over on Ketchem Street. They're here. They were on the bus with me."

He asks me how I know them, why they came down and everything else. He's very suspicious. I tell him the whole story about taking them to the doctor in my cab. He thinks it over. He's probably thinking that this is too much of a coincidence. But he says to the girl, "Five people would be safe. Especially with old people like that. They wouldn't try anything if there were five of us."

She says, "They can follow us back to New York."

He says, "They can follow us but if we stick together they can't do anything. As long as there are people around they can't do anything. There'd be too big a fuss. Five could do it. But I've got to tell the Blitnises something. I've got to give them an excuse for why I'm going to the bank and why they have to stay with me. I could say it has to do with gambling money. She's always saying I shouldn't gamble. I can tell her I want to quit while I'm ahead and take my winnings home and I'll feel safer with a lot of people around me."

I'm looking at him like this is a Dave Winger I never saw before. Mister Clean Conscience is all of a sudden Mister

Expert Liar. It shows you what happens when people get into a tight spot. Croppe and Grenlily use him and squeeze him and now, because of that, he doesn't trust me and he's ready to tell any lie to protect himself.

We go looking for the Blitnises and naturally we find Mrs. Blitnis at a blackjack table. She takes one look, gets up, picks up her money, and throws her arms around Dave. "Mr. Winger! Mr. Winger!" she says. "What a pleasure to see you!" She steps back and looks him over. "Were you gambling again?" she says to him.

He says, "That's what I want to talk to you about. Is your husband here?"

We go find Harry and Dave tells them his story about quitting and taking his winnings home. They eat it up. Mrs. Blitnis says, "Let's go. We'll stay with you the whole way back to New York."

17

SO THERE WE GO, ALL FIVE OF US, ME, DAVE, KATHY, and the Blitnises, marching across Pacific Street to the bank. The limousine is still there. Dave moseys right up to it like a hero. This is very hypocritical because I know that Dave is afraid of Al and Sid. I don't blame him for that because, for one thing, Sid has a reputation. But I do blame him for acting like he's not afraid just because he's got the four of us with him. Al rolls down the window. Dave says, "How long have you guys been here?"

Al says, "What is this? A delegation?"

Dave says, "They're my friends. They're coming to the bank with me."

Al gets out of the car and says, "Dave, I'm your friend. Ain't I your friend? Count me in. Where your friends go, I go." Then he looks at me. "Hey, Russ," he says, "why'd you run away?"

I say, "My hat blew off."

He says, "You need exercise, man. You look funny running like that. Driving that cab is making you a lard-ass."

I'm telling the story straight. I don't hide anything. I don't try to make myself look good. I'm an honest man, which these guys aren't.

Then he starts buttering up Kathy. He says, "Kathy, you are as beautiful in your coat here in Atlantic City as you were when I saw you in a lovelier costume, which I will not speak of here. I've been talking to people about you. People are interested. I'm ready to make appointments."

She says, "Who have you been talking to?"

He says, "Not now. We'll talk in private."

The man is a total, hundred percent liar but people believe him. I am believed less when I tell the truth than he is when he's lying.

Mrs. Blitnis is watching him and she says, "Who is this man?" Dave makes introductions all around. Now everybody knows everybody else's name but nobody knows anything about the people themselves that they didn't know before.

Al says, "Let's not stand around in the cold. We've got business. Let's go to the bank." But he doesn't go to the bank. He goes to the limo and gets an attaché case out of the back seat. Sid General watches all this from behind the wheel but he doesn't get out of the car.

We go to the bank. It's a very old place, very fancy but run down, left over from when Atlantic City was "The Playground of the World." In those days people came from all over for vacations here. The bank is marble—floors, walls, everything, all marble—but old and beat up, dirt washed into every vein and corner. Gold railings, gold bars on the tellers' windows, but the gold is wearing off and you can see the gray underneath. We go downstairs. A big, wide staircase made of white marble but it's so old that the steps have grooves in them from all the walking up and down. We go to the cage where they have the safe deposit boxes. Same thing—gold bars with the gold worn off. Old marble. An old lady is sitting in the cage and a guard is outside sitting at a table reading the paper. Dave signs so he can get his box. The old lady opens the gate and he's about to go in when Al says, "What are you going to put it in?"

Dave stops. He never thought of that. He's got forty-five thousand dollars in hundred-dollar bills. That's four hundred and fifty bills. It's not going to fit in his pockets. Al holds up the attaché case. Dave says, "Can I borrow that?"

Al says, "Borrow? I bought it for you. It's a gift. Come on. I'll show you how it works," and he goes into the cage ahead of Dave and says to the old lady, "We're together."

Dave doesn't want him in there but Al is already in. He's leading the way. We watch them go and then we stand there and wait.

Mrs. Blitnis says to me, "Were you gambling?"

I say, "No."

She says, "Good. Take my advice and don't gamble. Look at me. I have a system for blackjack but even I don't always win. My system needs time to work itself out. It can take all day. If I play all day, I win. But you came and interrupted me so I didn't have time. I don't know yet if the system worked or not."

Mr. Blitnis says, "What do you mean? If you have less money than you started with the system didn't work. If you have more it worked. What's the question?"

She says, "The system requires a full day. I can't judge from one hour's playing time."

He says, "Systems don't work." And they get into an argument.

I say to Kathy, "Did Dave decide what he's going to do about the lawyer?"

She looks at me like if she talked to me she'll get warts on her face. She turns around and walks away. Mr. Blitnis says to me, "That is some beauty. Is this Mr. Winger's girlfriend?"

Mrs. Blitnis says, "How long does Mr. Winger know her?"

I say, "A couple of weeks."

She says, "He'll be sorry for it. I'm not his mother. I can't warn him about everything. But if he likes this girl he's not as smart as I thought he was."

Kathy walks around the bank and we stand there talking about her. Finally Dave and Al come out. Dave is carrying the attaché case.

Al says, "All right, everybody. It's time for a celebration. I'm treating to dinner."

Dave says, "I'm sorry. We have to get back to New York."

Mr. Blitnis says, "We have time. The bus doesn't leave till six."

Dave says, "I got a car. I'll take you back in the car."

Mr. Blitnis says, "All the better. Then we don't have to worry about time. Let's join the man. Let's be festive. Eat, drink, and be merry. Then we'll drive back."

Al slaps Mr. Blitnis on the back. He says, "I like this man! 'Eat, drink, and be merry.' That's Shakespeare. Am I right? The Bard of London."

Blitnis says, "No, it's in the Declaration of Independence."

Al says, "You're right! I remember it now. My friend, we have a lot to talk about. I see you are also a lover of poetry."

Mr. Blitnis says, "I was in the grocery business for thirty-seven years."

Al says, "I want you to sit next to me. We'll talk about poetry. I'll give you some quotes and see if you can identify them. How's that? We'll have a contest. And I've got a great restaurant for it. A poetic restaurant."

Dave says, "Considering what I've got in this attaché case I don't think it's a good idea for me to go anyplace except right back to New York."

Meanwhile Kathy has come back to where we are. Al says to Kathy, "Kathy, help me out. I want everybody to get in the limo and come to the best restaurant in the world—my treat, in my limo, right now. How does that sound?"

She says, "It sounds great."

He says, "And we have something to talk about."

Dave says, "We have to get back to New York."

Al says, "Dave, it's safe. I guarantee it. Sid, my blood brother, will stand at the door of the restaurant and stop any dangerous characters."

Kathy thinks this is funny, but Dave is annoyed. Al says, "Listen, Dave, I'm serious. I understand why you're worried. But there won't be any trouble. I've got the ultimate guarantee. I don't like to mention this but Sid is armed. He's licensed and he knows how to use it. Believe me, with him protecting you, you are safe. If anybody acts suspicious, Sid will be there. I give you my personal guarantee that you will have that case and all its contents when you get back to New York."

Dave is not happy but Kathy is dying to go with Al. We all want to go. I also have money in my pocket, although nobody knows about it, but I want to go too. Whatever else you say about him, Al is a big spender. So why shouldn't I go? When else do I get a chance for a free meal in a first-class restaurant? Dave's the only one who doesn't want to go. He happens to be right but we're not interested in that so Dave has to give in.

We get in the limo, Kathy, Croppe, and Mrs. Blitnis in the back seat, Dave and me on the jump seats, and Mr. Blitnis up front with Sid. What Mr. Blitnis does up there I don't know. We start. Al takes out glasses, puts in ice from this little refrigerator, and pours whiskey-and-sodas for everybody. He says, "I propose a toast. Let's drink to what we're all here for—money."

Kathy laughs. "I'll drink to that," she says, and we all drink.

Al says, "But man does not live by bread alone. Let's toast to pleasure." And we all drink to pleasure.

Mrs. Blitnis is feeling it already. She says, "I also propose a toast. I propose a toast to Mr. Winger."

Al says, "I second that. To Dave Winger. A great guy." And we all drink to Dave Winger. "What else?" Al says.

Mrs. Blitnis says, "To life."

Al says, "To life!" And we all drink to life.

Dave says, "How far is it to this restaurant?"

Al says, "To the restaurant!" and we all drink to the restaurant.

Al pours more whiskey and soda. "Don't let the well run dry," he says.

Kathy says, "Let's make a night of it!"

Al says, "Yes, 'I burn a candle on both the ends.' That's Harriet Beecher Stowe. Let's drink to Harriet Beecher Stowe." We all drink to Harriet Beecher Stowe.

Al opens the glass partition to the front and yells up to Mr. Blitnis, "How about, 'I burn a candle on both the ends'? You know that one?" he says.

Mr. Blitnis says, "Of course I know it. It's a famous poem. William Butler Yeats. 'I burn a candle on both my ends.' Who doesn't know that poem?"

Al slams the partition shut. He says, "We are going to the best Italian restaurant in the United States of America."

Dave says, "Where is it?"

Al says, "Are you telling me you don't know where to find the best Italian restaurant in the United States of America? A restaurant written up in every guidebook? Internationally famous. People from all over the world lining up to get in. Where else would you look? There's only one place. And I am known personally to the owner. Luigi. I am going to order directly and personally from the owner. The meal of a lifetime. Twelve courses. Wine with every course. But we got time. We need another toast. Fill up the glasses!"

Mrs. Blitnis says, "No, thank you. I got plenty. It's a good thing Harry is up front. He's got a gallbladder and he shouldn't drink."

I look out the window. We're rolling down a highway. I can't tell how fast we're going because it's such a big, smooth-riding car but we're passing everything else on the road.

Dave says, "Where are you taking us, Al?"

Al says, "David, my friend, I want you to know that whatever I do I do out of love. That's why I do things in the City of Brotherly Love. You will love it there. The best Italian restaurants in the world are in South Philadelphia. A toast to brotherly love!"

Dave is upset and he's angry. Maybe he feels a little stupid because Al tricked him again. This is further than any of us expected to go. At first, when I heard it, I was upset too. But I figure, what's the difference? I got time. Dave's got a car to drive us back to New York. This is all on the house so why not enjoy it? I have another drink. I'm in a limo, I've got a thousand dollars in one pocket, three rolls of quarters in the other, and for once in my life I'm ahead of the game. I sit back and I'm feeling pretty good.

18

I EXPECTED A BIG, FANCY PLACE BUT IT WAS SO small we had to wait in line for a table. Croppe said it was world famous but it didn't look like much to me. There must be something to the place because the line waiting for tables kept getting longer. Normally, I will not stand in line for anything. Life is too short for long lines. I work twelve hours a day, five days a week. How much of my spare time do you think I'm willing to put in standing in line? But here I got no choice. We got to this restaurant at four o'clock in the afternoon, which is early for dinner, and there's already a line. But it's not as long as it gets later and we don't have a big wait.

Sid stays in the car. The man never gets out of the car. Dave holds on to the attaché case like he thinks everybody else is working on a plan to steal it. Al has Kathy off to the side and he's whispering to her and they're laughing. This makes Dave unhappy but he doesn't do anything about it.

Finally we get a table. Right away Croppe gets into this big discussion with the waiter. It's so involved that the waiter calls over two other guys. All these guys are wearing black jackets and black bow ties. I don't know if one of them's the owner or not and I don't care. Al can tell me any story he wants as long as he's picking up the tab. The four of them discuss what we're going to eat. They go into every detail—sauces, salads, dressings, cooked in oil, browned in butter, turned over once, turned over twice, details about food I never heard discussed before. Then they get to the wines. Red, white, heavy, light, aroma, and I don't know what else. They go on for twenty minutes. Croppe orders for all of us, which is fine with me.

The three guys in black jackets are not the ones who bring out the food. They got two other guys in brown jackets to do that. And the two guys in brown jackets don't take the dishes away after we finish. They got a guy in a white jacket to do that. It's like a union shop where everybody does a quarter of the job. It takes seven of them to wait on six of us.

The first thing they bring us is this little brown fritter with a white sauce. The waiter in the black coat comes over and announces what this is but I don't remember what he called it. We also get a white wine. When we finish, the guy in the white coat takes away the dishes and the guys in brown coats come back and bring us each a plate of salad with slices of cheese and salami and stuff like that with a lot of oil and vinegar. The waiter in black makes an announcement again about what it's called. He announces every dish like this is the ballet. We finish it and the guy in the white coat takes away the dishes and the guys in brown coats come back and bring us this little piece of cold fish. We eat the fish and then we get chicken livers and another wine. Then they bring out a hot dish of shrimp with a lot of garlic which looks to me like it's the main meal after a lot of little appetizers. The waiter in the black coat announces that this is "shrimp scampi del Greco." It tastes a lot better than it sounds. The guys in brown serve it and we also get a white wine. It's all been small portions but there was a lot of them and they were all good and there was garlic bread too so now I'm full. We're splitting each of these wine bottles six ways so we each get only one or two glasses but we're getting so many bottles that it adds up to a lot and I'm also pretty drunk. The guy in the white coat takes away the dishes and I'm ready for dessert but instead, here come the guys in brown coats and the waiter is announcing, "Baked Campagna capon stuffed with oyster del Torino and pasta side dish." This is another whole meal which I wasn't expecting. Croppe said twelve courses but I didn't pay attention because I don't believe anything Croppe says. I'm already full but I eat the chicken and wash it down with two glasses of white wine. Now I'm really stuffed like a pig. The guy in the white coat takes away the chicken and pretty soon the waiter is back with the guys in brown coats and he announces, "Veal medallions in cream sauce with pearl onions." A medallion is the metal thing they attach to the hood of a Yellow cab. Naturally I realize this is something else entirely but I don't know why they use the same word. This veal dish is another full meal. When I finish it and the wine that comes with it I'm filled to the gills. And by the way, each wine is also a performance. Every time the guy brings out a bottle he shows it to Al before he opens it. I don't know what Al knows about wine but he acts like he's an expert. He reads the label and gives the waiter a nod. The waiter pulls the cork with his corkscrew and pours a little bit in Al's glass. Al sniffs it, takes a sip, thinks about it, and says, *"Bellissimo!"* or *"Muy bien!"* because you have to talk about wines in a foreign language. The waiter gets all excited every time Al approves, as if he never expected to get approval from such a big expert like Al, and he gives him a big "Aha!" or *"Bellissimo!"* right back like this is the best news he's had in a long time. Then he pours for everybody.

We finish the veal, they take away the dishes, and before we know it they're back. "Beef à la Roma," the guy announces and they bring us this meat dish with vegetables, another whole meal and another wine, this time red. I lost track of what number course we're up to now but I'm hoping we're near the end. I force this meat into my mouth but, believe me, I don't enjoy it. It's just that you hate to leave it over when you know that tomorrow, when you're very hungry and eating a hamburger someplace, you'll curse yourself for not eating this when you had it in front of you for free. By the time I finish, the food has no taste. The place is starting to feel like a steam bath. I'm sweating. There's no air. I loosen my belt and the button on my pants. My stomach is so swollen I have to unzip my fly to make room. I even have to untie my shoelaces because my feet are swollen. When I bend to loosen my laces it feels like my stomach is going to bust open.

Now they're taking away the meat dishes and I'm praying it's all over. I look around and see Mr. Blitnis is sound asleep. Mrs. Blitnis has got the meat cut into tiny bits and she's still forcing food into her mouth with her pinky sticking out. Dave started with the attaché case on his lap but after a while he slipped it down out of sight under the table between his feet. He's young, he's got an appetite, but even he is finished. Kathy is leaning on his shoulder and smiling with her eyes shut like she's drunk. Sid is out in the car. They brought food out to him but I don't think he's eating like us.

Croppe gets up and walks around the table. "Everybody happy?" he says. "Anybody need anything?" He goes over to Blitnis and says, "Look at this guy! He's snoring! Hey, Mr. Blitnis! This is a feast. Let's have some poetry!" And he starts shaking him.

Blitnis wakes up but for a couple of seconds he doesn't know where he is.

Mrs. Blitnis says, "Let him sleep. This kind of meal is no good for him. He's got a gallbladder. Better he should sleep than eat this. He needs stale food. That's a doctor's orders."

Blitnis figures out where he is and says, "I'm under a doctor's orders."

Croppe says, "Gallbladder? Why don't you have it out?"

Blitnis says, "Not so fast. It's not a casual thing to cut open a stomach."

Croppe says, "Are you kidding me? They have a new operation for gallbladder. They do it in one day. In and out. I had both my gallbladders out and look at me. I can eat anything. Fit as a fiddle. Guess my age."

Mr. Blitnis says, "My doctor is one of the biggest surgeons on the east coast. He's taken out more gallbladders than all the other surgeons combined. He says, 'Diet first,' and if he says diet, I diet."

Croppe says, "Mr. Blitnis, gallbladder was cured in 1965. They got a simple operation. It's all done with computers. Your doctor doesn't know what he's talking about."

Blitnis says, "Mr. Croppe, my doctor is the biggest expert on gallbladder in the United States."

Croppe says, "Who told you that?"

Blitnis says, "Nobody told me that. I know for myself. I know doctors. You should hear how my doctor talks to his nurses—like they're dirt."

Croppe says, "Mr. Blitnis, I won't argue with you. I can see that you think for yourself. Just take my card in case you change your mind. I can make all the arrangements and you'll be in and out in one day. You won't even have a scar because they use a laser beam. And I'll tell you what else I can do. I'll get you a kickback on your Medicare. And it's all

legal. But this is a feast so let's forget gallbladder. Let's have
some poetry. You know any drinking poems? You know the
one about, 'A bunch of verses beneath the bell—'?"

Mr. Blitnis says, "Of course I know it. It's a very famous
poem. It's by an ancient Persian rugmaker, Omar Khay-
yám."

Croppe says, "Okay. Good. Let's hear it."

Blitnis says, "I don't have the memory I used to. I was in
the grocery business thirty-seven years."

Croppe says, "In that case, let's have dessert."

They bring out pastry. I never saw pastry like that before.
Every one of them looked delicious. But I couldn't eat any-
thing. I couldn't take one bite. To this day it bothers me that
I left all that pastry without tasting a single one of them.

19

WHILE CROPPE SETTLES THE BILL I GET UP AND GO outside. It's dark out now. Sweat is pouring off me. I stand out in the street and it's maybe twenty degrees but it feels good. Then they all come out. We get in the limo and head back to Atlantic City. Everybody's moaning and groaning about their stomachs and their heads. The car is warm, the seat is comfortable, and in no time I'm sound asleep. I don't know anything, I don't see anything, I don't hear anything, and I don't know how long I been sleeping. All of a sudden there's a big ruckus and I wake up. Dave is arguing with Al. He's yelling, "I left it there! I'm telling you I left it there! We have to go back!"

You know how when you go someplace to do something and you do everything but that? Or when you want to tell somebody something and you talk to them for two hours and tell them everything but what you meant to? The thing that's most on your mind is what you forget. It happens to everybody. So just imagine if you're dealing with an irresponsible kid like Dave Winger. It's his briefcase, it's got his money in it, but he leaves it there. And now he's half crazy and yelling and Al is talking calm to him, which is making him even crazier.

Al says, "Don't get excited. Getting excited won't help. Let's stop at a phone and call them."

Dave says, "I'll use this phone." Because there's a phone right in the car.

Al says, "You can't. It don't work."

Dave yells, "Then turn around! We have to go back!"

Al says, "Let's be sensible. You say you left it there and I believe you. You're the only one who touched it so you must know. You didn't want anybody else to lay a hand on it. But if you left it there, either they have it or they don't. Am I right? Whoever sat there after us either turned it in or they kept it. That's been done. It's decided. There's nothing you can do now. So stay calm. You can't change what already happened."

I thought Dave was going to start banging his head against the window. But I couldn't believe what he did. This is a boy who seems intelligent but he can't keep himself straight. He's always got to do something stupid. First he gets in-

volved with this con man. Then, even after he realizes he's
been used, he lets this same con man talk him into going to
Philadelphia to eat dinner when he's carrying an attaché case
with forty-five thousand dollars in it. He should have
headed straight home with that money. Then he leaves it in
the restaurant. Just like he let Al keep the check for fifty
thousand in the first place. Where is his head? He's like a
baby.

While they're talking I see the exit sign for Atlantic City.
That means I must have slept for an hour. We pull off the
highway and Sid stops at a phone. Dave jumps out, gets
information, and calls Philly. He can hardly stand still. He
gets the restaurant and asks if they saw a brown attaché
case. He's so excited he has trouble explaining himself and
they don't know what he's talking about. Finally he makes it
clear and they say to hold on and they'll look for it. He holds
on a while and they come back and tell him, "No briefcase."
He goes nuts and goes through the whole thing again. He's
yelling, "Not a briefcase. An attaché case." They tell him,
"No case. No case of any kind."

He comes to the car and says, "We have to go back. We
have to go back."

Believe me, the way I felt I didn't want to go back. I
wanted to go home and get to bed. But we had to go back. So
we turn around and we're on the road going in the opposite
direction, back to Philly. Now nobody can sleep. Everybody's uncomfortable. We doze, wake up, doze, wake up
again. Everybody has to go to the bathroom. The longer
we're riding the worse it gets and the worse it gets the more

awake and grouchier everybody gets. Pretty soon there are a lot of nasty things being said to Dave because it's his fault we're still in the car instead of in a clean bathroom in one of the casinos. Even Kathy is nasty to him. By this time she's figured out that he's not rich—although maybe she's wrong about that, we still can't be sure what his parents in Ohio are like. But she doesn't think about that. Probably all she's thinking about now is that Croppe is going to make her a world-famous model.

Finally we get to the restaurant and we all head for the bathroom—except Dave. He starts checking tables. He's like a nut, looking under tables and chairs, asking people if they saw a brown attaché case. The guys in black jackets are following him around, smiling at everybody with these stupid-looking smiles because they're helpless. They're apologizing all over the place, very embarrassed because they can't stop him and they don't know what he'll do next.

When I come out of the bathroom I feel better. It shows you what nature is. There's forty-five thousand dollars missing, Dave Winger, who's supposed to be my friend, is just about ruined, but all I know is that I'm mad at him because my bladder is full. When I come out of the bathroom, I'm a totally different person. I feel sorry for him again.

When I was in the bathroom alone I got a look at my thousand dollars, which I hadn't seen since they gave it to me. I knew it was in my pocket because I could feel it, but this was all so crazy that I was getting a little worried that I only imagined I won the money. When I pulled out that wad and saw the hundred-dollar bills I felt better.

By now Dave has looked everywhere, even the coat room and the kitchen, but he can't believe it. I help him look again. We look in places two and three times but it's not there. The money is gone.

So here he is in Philadelphia and everybody's looking at him like he's crazy. He came to New York with this idea of helping people. Instead, he winds up passing bad checks in Atlantic City. He owes a bank fifty thousand dollars plus interest. He had forty-five thousand in an attaché case that gave him a chance to pay it back but he left the money under the table in the restaurant. The man he trusted most, Al Croppe, is a crook. He's being charged with a crime, he's going on trial, and his lawyer is a crook. And he can't even pay this lawyer. He can't do anything.

We get back in the car and he looks like a dead man. Sid starts it up and we pull out. I shut my eyes and I don't say anything. Al is kidding with Kathy and she's laughing. I open my eyes and look at them. I see the three of them, Al, Dave, and Kathy, and you'd think any girl her age would go for Dave without a second thought. But she's cuddling up with Al who has to be at least twice her age and they're both laughing. Dave is alone, looking out the window.

Sid drives us to where Dave is parked in Atlantic City. Dave gets out and he expects Kathy to come with him but she says, "Dave, I think I'm going to ride back with Al."

Al says, "Listen, Dave, I don't want you to worry. You and I are friends and Al Croppe does not leave his friends high and dry. You're not lost yet. Get that chin up. Meet me at the Green Leaf tomorrow at six, we'll have dinner and we'll work something out. Meanwhile, you need a clear head. I'll take everybody home and you go by yourself so you can think."

Al slams the door, Kathy blows him a kiss, and we pull out. Dave is standing by his car looking at us.

I say, "Al. Stop the car."

He says, "What for?"

I say, "I'm going back with Dave. I don't want him to drive all that way alone."

He says, "Forget it. He needs time by himself. It'll clear his mind." And we keep going.

The whole way back Al and Kathy are cuddling up together. It makes me sick.

It shows you how desperate Dave was that at six o'clock the next day he came to the Green Leaf looking for Al Croppe. He's got nobody else to turn to.

Since my shift ends at six, I was also there. I sat at the bar and had a cup of coffee. No alcohol for me. I'm barely over my headache. I was so stuffed all that day that I didn't eat but by the time I got to the Green Leaf I was hungry, which is exactly what I knew would happen. I'm sitting at the bar in this grease joint remembering beef à la Roma, veal medallions, and the pastry which I never touched, which were all free and which I couldn't enjoy because I was so stuffed and which now, if I could have any one of them, would be a very nice meal. But if I'm going to eat now I've got to shell out my own money, which I don't want to do since I missed a day's work and things will be very tight this week. I'm not counting the thousand dollars in my pocket because I don't want to fritter it away. I didn't even give Brenda her five hundred yet. I'm still thinking about that because it's going to be something special. I'm not going to just plunk it down on the kitchen table. I want to do it in a way that she'll always remember. Believe me, I enjoyed thinking about it. As they say, anticipation is as good as the real thing. So I'm walking around with the thousand dollars rolled up in my pocket and every once in a while, when I'm in a bathroom or someplace where it's private, I take a look at it.

From where I'm sitting at the bar I can see Al and Dave at a table and they're talking. Al is talking. Dave is listening and shaking his head, no, no, no. This goes on for a long time. My coffee gets cold. Finally Al gets up and leaves. I wait a few minutes and then I go over and sit down with Dave. Al didn't finish his french fries so I eat them. I wouldn't normally do that but I didn't want to spend any money and I was hungry and he didn't put any ketchup on them or do anything to make them disgusting. Dave is watching but he doesn't say anything. He's in such bad shape that he doesn't realize what I'm doing. I say, "Did Al have any ideas for you?"

He says, "He wants me to declare bankruptcy."

I say, "What'll that do?"

He says, "That means they sell your assets and divide the money up to all the people you owe and they take whatever it comes to as full payment."

I say, "What assets do you have?"

He says, "I don't have any assets. If I declare bankruptcy,

that's it. The bank is stuck. They write it off as a bad debt."

I say, "Sounds like a good deal."

He says, "I think he's got that briefcase."

I say, "It wouldn't surprise me."

I didn't think of it before but now that he mentions it, it makes sense. Al must have spent five, six hundred dollars at that restaurant. Why would he do that? If he knew we'd all get so boozed up and sleepy and dazed that he could just lift the attaché case, it would make sense. It was probably in the trunk of the car the whole time we were riding back and forth. I said, "What are you going to do?"

He says, "What choice do I have?"

I say, "How do you declare bankruptcy? Maybe I'll do it myself."

He says, "Al is going to have his lawyer arrange it."

I said, "You mean Grenlily? The guy who's supposed to get you off in Atlantic City?"

He nods.

I say, "Doesn't it occur to you that you're getting in deeper and deeper?"

He says, "What do you think I'm so upset about?"

So I say, "Then why do you go on with it?"

He says, "What do you suggest?"

I'm stumped. I got no suggestions. The guy is trapped.

20

MEANWHILE, I HAD MY OWN PROBLEMS BECAUSE when I got back from Atlantic City it was around midnight, which is five hours later than I usually get home from work and I didn't have any money. I'm not counting that thousand dollars. It took a lot of will-power not to use that thousand, not even to mention it, because there was no money in the house until I earned some the next day. I told Brenda that I got so sick I had to go to the hospital. I told her they kept me for ob-servation in Elmhurst Hospital all day. I said I was so dizzy I couldn't even make a phone call. The way I looked you could believe it. I

had a headache, a stomachache, and I'd been sleeping in the
limousine for hours. I think she believed me when I told her
the story but the next day I could see that she thought it over
and didn't believe it any more. I wasn't worried. I figured
when I pulled out those five hundred-dollar bills and gave
them to her there'd be no more questions. Questions are not
a problem from Brenda anyway. When I tell her something,
she accepts it. I think she knows I lie to her sometimes, but
she knows I never lie about anything important. I wouldn't
do that. Brenda is a good person and I couldn't do that to her.

Maybe I should have just given her the five hundred right
away. Maybe I shouldn't have made such a fuss over it. To
some people a thousand dollars isn't much. Here's Dave
with fifty thousand, Al Croppe fooling around with hundreds of thousands, and even people like the Blitnises must
have a big bank account because they're retired and still
living nicely. But I never had a thousand dollars in my
pocket before and I don't think I ever will again so to me it's
a lot of money and I wanted to get full satisfaction out of it. I
didn't want to dribble it away. I wanted to do something so
special that after it was done I could say, "If I had another
thousand, I'd do the same thing over again." I never even
thought of keeping it all to myself. Right from the start I
wanted to give Brenda half. The only reason I didn't was
because I couldn't think of the right way to do it. This was a
once-in-a-lifetime thing.

All that week I had to hustle because I was trying to make
five days' pay in four days. I'm driving fast and all the time
I'm thinking about what to do with that thousand dollars. I

was afraid I'd never think of anything good enough. It's like if you had just one wish. It was making me crazy. To show you how crazy I got, I started to wish I didn't have the money. But that was only a little part of the time. The rest of the time I was thinking just the opposite. I was wishing for more. Before this I was never a greedy person. I could have made more money in a different job but I liked being free, out in the open, on the streets, and that was important to me. But once I had that thousand, a thousand wasn't enough. I was afraid that as soon as I spent it I'd realize that I spent it on the wrong thing. What I needed was another thousand. If I could have another thousand then I'd feel easier about spending the original thousand. I wouldn't feel that it had to be perfect or that I couldn't make a mistake. So I'm debating with myself. Where can I get more money? Should I take, say, fifty dollars and buy lottery tickets? But the odds are so bad that fifty dollars doesn't mean anything in the lottery. Some people spend fifty dollars a week on lottery tickets and don't win. I'd have to risk five hundred or the whole thousand.

One day I'm walking home and my head is full of this kind of thing and who do I run into but Al Croppe. I don't keep the same hours as Al Croppe so I don't often run into him. When I see him now it strikes me as strange and I get suspicious. This is what happens when you've got money on your mind. You get suspicious and cagey. My first thought is, What's he doing here? But I gave him a nice hello, which is hypocritical, because I don't like him and I know he don't like me. And he gives me a nice hello back and walks along with me. I don't remember what we were talking about because the whole time I had on my mind that maybe this is an opportunity I should take advantage of and I'm afraid he'll leave me before I get a chance to. Finally I say, "By the way, Al, have you done the sheets lately?"

He says, "Where'd you hear about the sheets?"

I say, "You told me."

He says, "I don't do the sheets any more."

I say, "You told me you pick winners nine out of ten times."

He says, "That's absolutely true. But what's the payoff? My time is too valuable to spend on that kind of payoff. Russ, let me ask you something. I wouldn't ask this but, since you bring it up, do you ever think of that? What your time is worth?"

I say, "I work twelve hours a day, five days a week."

He says, "That's what I'm talking about. You put in sixty hours for less than most guys make in forty."

I'm insulted but I swallow it. You swallow things if you smell money. I say to him, "Well, the fact is I could use some extra money."

He says, "Sure. We all could. But the sheets are small time. It's no way to make money. Russ, let me tell you something. You impressed me down there in Atlantic City. I realized that maybe I been misunderestimating you. I found out what happened. I found out you took a day off and went down there out of loyalty to a friend. That's very impressive. There's not ten guys in a thousand that would do it."

I know Al Croppe is a liar, a con man, and everything else

but I appreciated him saying that. Dave Winger never showed any appreciation for what I did. In fact, Dave was suspicious. Even after his girlfriend dumped him he never dropped the suspicion she put in his head.

Al says, "I'll be honest with you, Russ. It made me sit up and take notice. I know what you think of me and I won't try to convince you different but I want you to know one thing. No matter what you think of me, I am an honest business-man. I am a businessman who operates on handshakes and word of honor, not written contracts. I don't trust written contracts. My word is my bond. When I see a man who is loyal, whose word is his bond, a man like me, I take an interest in him. That's what I liked about you. It was an act of honor. I'll tell you something—I don't knock what a man does for a living but I believe that you are not working up to your abilities. You could do a lot better than drive a cab. You got a little time?" he says. "I'd like to talk to you. Let's go in and have dinner."

We're in front of this nice restaurant and I know he's going to pick up the tab so how can I say no?

We go in and make ourselves comfortable and he says to me, "Russ, people have funny ideas about what is business. They don't realize that business is war. In war the idea is to win. If you're about to get killed you don't think about rules. You think about how to survive. The same in sports. Each team wants to win. On television it looks like they're fol-lowing the rules but down on the field they're doing every-thing they can get away with. They're doing it behind the ref's back or so the umpire won't see it but you and I know they're doing it. And they got to because their livelihood's at stake. It's the same in business. You understand me? Now I'm an entrepen-ewer. My idea is to go out and make a buck. There's no other reason to be in business. It's not a charity. Now where do you make a buck? I'll tell you. The buck is made in the marketplace. And the marketplace is open to everybody. Everybody has an equal chance in the market-place. It's free and democratic. The market don't look for who's good or who's bad. It don't look for crooked or hon-est. All it looks for is the buck. That's a philosophy that goes back to a man named Adam Smith. I don't know if you know anything about philosophy or economics but this Adam Smith invented the free market and he ran the first free market in the world someplace in England. He set up rules which haven't been changed to this day. It shows you what kind of a genius the man was. Do you understand what I'm telling you?"

I say, "Sure, Al, I understand." And I do. I understand a lot of things. I see right through him. I know he's leading up to something. He don't care about philosophy or marketplace or anything else except making money. A few weeks ago I would not have sat there. But things have changed because, liar though he is, I know he don't lie about the amount of money he deals with. I've seen proof of that. So I sit there and listen to him. He says, "What is it you want, Russ? You say you're looking for some extra money. What kind of money do you have in mind?"

I'm too embarrassed to say a thousand dollars. I say, "I could use about five hundred."

He says, "Do you know about the exchange Dave Winger worked with the hotel in Atlantic City?"

I say, "I have an idea."

He says, "It's a very simple system. I deposit money in a bank in your name. But everything, even your name, has my signature. You go to a casino. They fill out a card on your checking account to allow you to cash checks. They're not worried because they got you right there. You're a guest in the hotel. I write checks and I sign your name. You cash the checks I wrote as if you wrote them. Then I take the money out of the bank and the checks bounce. The casino has you arrested. You say nothing. You plead not guilty. You go to court. Donnie Grenlily is your lawyer. He asks you to show your driver's license, your ID. He even shows the hotel registration card. All these things have your signature and your signature is nothing like the one on the checks. So why are they blaming you? The cashier says you cashed them but it's his word against yours and one against one won't convict. That's in the United States Constitution. So the judge throws the case out of court. But we say we don't want it thrown out. We want an acquittal. We get an acquittal and then we sue the hotel for false arrest and deflamation of character. They don't want court cases like that so they settle out of court. We keep what we got for the checks plus maybe another hundred, two hundred thousand, maybe even a quarter of a million in damages.

"Now, with Dave, I never laid it all out for him because he couldn't handle it. I had to lead him step by step. With you, it's different. You're smart. You can handle it. I tell you the whole deal. I lay it out for you and let you decide from the beginning if you want to do it."

I say, "What's going to happen to Dave?"

He says, "As soon as he agrees to sue the hotel he's going to be okay. He's just got to sign some papers for Donnie Grenlily."

I say, "What about this guy Grenlily? I thought you said he messed you up."

"Russ," he says, "Donnie and me go back a long way. Sometimes I say things. It's all in the game. You understand me?"

I say, "Is Dave going to go bankrupt?"

He says, "Let me give you a piece of advice, Russ. I have a rule—if you don't know, don't ask. If you need to know something, somebody will tell you. Dave Winger will be taken care of. Dave Winger could have made himself a lot of money but he acts like a little boy. He talks like a little boy. Nobody hurts a little boy but nobody gives him money either. You understand me? That's all you need to know. Now let's talk about you. Are you ready for a trip to Atlantic City?"

I know that no matter how simple he makes it sound this is big trouble. I also know that it is illegal. It's not just illegal, it's crooked. And I know that if I touch it, I'm putting myself in Al Croppe's hands. I say to him, "That's not in my line of work."

He says, "Your share is twenty-five thousand in cash."

When I heard that my mouth must have fallen open.

He says to me, "This is not illegal. Nobody gets hurt. Nobody gets hit on the head. We do exactly the same thing the casinos do. People go down there to gamble but that's not really gambling. The casinos aren't gambling because the casinos set the odds. They make themselves automatic winners. All we do is reverse the procedure. We set the odds so we win. You follow what I'm saying?"

I don't follow what Al Croppe is saying. It doesn't matter what Al Croppe is saying. I know better than to listen to Al Croppe. But I'm being honest here so I'll tell you the truth. Al does not have to convince me. Once I heard twenty-five thousand dollars I can't turn it down.

21

IF YOU GO TO THE RACETRACK AND HIT THE DAILY double, a really big daily double, for a couple of weeks you'll have money in your pocket. You hit a football pool and you can make a day's pay. But twenty-five thousand dollars is different. That's like hitting the lottery. The odds on the lottery are in the millions but people play it because if you hit the lottery it changes your life. That's what twenty-five thousand dollars meant to me. It was like offering me a college education. With that much cash I could do something. I could start my own business. I could take the time to find a really good job. So how could I turn it down? What would I turn it down for? So I could keep driving a cab?

Dave already told me the whole story of his time in Atlantic City. Every detail. That gave me a reference, something I could use to check what Al was telling me. I never trust Al but, in this case, because I knew Dave's story, I knew Al was telling the truth. I knew the whole deal ahead of time. So I'm not afraid of Al.

I knew it was not legal. I knew it was wrong. But I figured it was only a matter of four or five days, one very quick thing, in and out, and after that I'd have money. I'd be respectable. I could set myself up. I could breathe. So I told him I'd do it.

Just like Dave, we started by going to that basement in Astoria for clothes. We had a different guy, not Freddie, a thin guy named John. I could see right off that Al was not trying to pull things on me that he pulled on Dave. He didn't try to get me to pay. I got suits, jackets, pants, shirts, handkerchiefs, socks, everything. I filled up two very expensive suitcases and Al paid for the whole thing—a hundred dollars.

I didn't have to sign for a bank loan or put up any money. Al went to the bank, opened the account, put in his money in my name. He used his signature and naturally the account was in a different bank. And I was going to a different hotel in Atlantic City. We were also going for less money—twenty-five thousand, five thousand a day for five days. Sid General knew the printing company that printed the checks so we didn't have to wait for them. And they were the official checks. Everything went very smooth. I didn't hit a problem until I got home carrying those two suitcases.

This was the second time in a week that I came home after midnight and Brenda was up waiting for me both times. She didn't know what to think when she saw the suitcases. She didn't believe my hospital story and she knew that last time I came back late I had no money to give her. But that's all she knew. I never told her I went to Atlantic City. And I still hadn't mentioned that thousand dollars. Now I walk in with these two fancy suitcases. I put them down and the first thing I do is lay the money I earned driving that day on the kitchen table. When she sees that she knows I worked. Whatever she was thinking, that throws her off. She's looking at the money and she's looking at the suitcases. She says to me, "Russ, are you doing something you shouldn't?"

I laugh. I say, "What makes you think that?" and I'm acting as if those suitcases don't exist.

She says, "You don't have to do anything like that. We can get by on what you make driving. We done it so far."

I say, "Brenda, what are you talking about? I've been driving all day. There's the money."

She says, "Russ, don't do anything wrong. Don't get in trouble. I need you here, with me."

I give her a big hug. There are a lot of people in the world who make a lot more money than me who never heard that from their wife. Nobody tells Al Croppe they need him. He could drop dead tomorrow and nobody would miss him. I was tempted to pull out those five hundred-dollar bills and give them to her right then and there. But I didn't because it would be insulting. It would be like paying her for what she said.

So the suitcases sit there in the living room and nobody mentions them. This is a very small apartment so you can't miss them. The kids come in, look at them, I mean really look at them, then they look at Brenda but they don't look at me. And they don't say anything. Not to me anyway. Maybe they ask Brenda when I'm not there but I don't hear it. The more time that goes by with nobody saying anything, the more everybody's thinking about the suitcases. Like they're getting bigger and bigger. I feel like every time somebody moves they have to walk around them. It's getting me crazy. I feel like I should say something. But if I say one word it'll open the door and there'll be no place to stop. I'll have to tell the whole story. I don't want to do that. Maybe afterwards I'll tell them, but I can't now.

It's a funny thing about having money. All money is the same. A dollar is a dollar no matter how you got it. If you stole it off a dead body, if you won it on a horse, or if you earned it digging ditches it all buys the same things and it all gets you the same respect. When I walk in the door with twenty-five thousand dollars and tell my family we're moving to a better apartment, we're buying clothes, we're going out to dinner, and I'm going into business, I'll be a hero. But if I tell them now, before I go, when I don't have the money, I won't get the same respect. I won't be like a guy who could have twenty-five thousand dollars so they'll try to talk me out of it. I didn't want to listen to that. So all night long the suitcases sit there and nobody says a word about them.

The next morning I don't get up at five the way I usually do for my six o'clock shift. Al was coming later to take me to the airport. I was flying to Atlantic City instead of Sid driving me in the limo. At 6 A.M. I'm still home so Brenda knows that whatever I'm doing, I'm doing it that day. After the kids left for school I got up, opened one of the suitcases, took out a brand-new suit, a shirt, a tie, and shoes. Brenda is staring at me like I'm Cinderella. I think she would have asked me about it then but she was dumbstruck. I got all dressed up and I looked like a million dollars. And there she is in her old torn nightgown. I gave her a hug and I said, "Don't worry. This is a legitimate business deal. I'll be back in five days and I'm gonna bring you a brand-new nightgown. And we're gonna make money this time."

She says, "Russ, I don't care about money or the night-gown. I just don't want you to do anything wrong. Do you know what I mean? Don't do anything wrong."

I say to her, "Brenda, I don't have to worry about that because you're good enough for both of us."

She says, "No I'm not. That's just talk. Take off the suit. Please. You can still go in and drive half a shift."

I laugh. At least I try to laugh. I say, "Five days and we're gonna be a lot better off than ever before. Trust me just this once."

She says, "Five days? How will we eat? I don't have money for five days."

I hadn't thought of that. I'm leaving her with one day's pay. That won't get her through five days. I'm going to have to borrow something from Croppe. I figure he'll give me an advance on the twenty-five thousand. In fact, seeing how he is with money, I figure that if I ask him for a hundred for my wife he'll probably give it as a gift. So I say to her, "I'm going to leave you enough money to get through. Just think of this as a business trip. Imagine your husband is a businessman. I'd go away all the time."

She says, "You're not a businessman. You're a cabdriver. My husband don't run around on trips with fancy suitcases. He stays home with me. Don't go, Russ."

I can't listen to this any more. I pick up the suitcases and head downstairs. When I get to the street I see the limo with Sid in front and Al in the back. I go over to them and Al opens the door. He starts right in talking, the way he always does, so you don't get a chance to think. He tells me to get in and before I know it I'm inside and we're heading for the airport. When I finally get a chance to say something, I say to him, "Al, look, this is embarrassing but I forgot to leave my wife enough cash until I'm back. Could you do me a favor? Would you give her a hundred dollars and take it out of my twenty-five thousand? It'd be a big favor."

He says, "Would I mind? Russ, baby, how could I mind? You got kids. I love kids. Is a hundred enough? How about I leave her two hundred? And listen, this does not come out of your share. This is on me."

So I got on the plane feeling good. It was my first plane ride and I went first class. I did everything first class, the whole five days. First class was part of the operation because I was supposed to look like a big spender. I got to Atlantic City, got my hotel room, my credit check, and rented a safe deposit box. The next day I cashed the first check, put away forty-five hundred, and had five hundred to gamble with. I was also carrying my original thousand which I won in the slot machine. Nobody knew I had it but I had no place to hide it so I always kept it with me.

A few days went by and it turned out to be different for me down there than it was for Dave Winger. At first I thought it was great. I felt good rubbing elbows with all those rich people and big spenders. Everything I ate, every place I went, I went first class. I really enjoyed myself.

Then one night, I guess it was about the third night, I go out on the boardwalk and I decide to walk down to the beach. People don't do that much because you get sand in your shoes. I'm a little nervous because it's dark out there and I have my thousand rolled up in one pocket and five hundred for tonight's gambling in the other. But generally I was feeling very good. I just had a nice meal. I was sleeping late every day. I was relaxing. This was the first real vacation I ever had. I had vacations where you took a few days off but I never had one where you went away. So I'm really enjoying myself. I'm walking down on the beach and I can hear the waves breaking, louder and louder as I get near the water. Finally I'm standing right at the ocean. If I get any closer my shoes will get wet. I stand there and listen to the waves. It's an odd thing but it's almost like I have in mind that I'll just stand there and listen until the waves stop. Naturally I know they'll never stop. Any idiot knows that. But I never really thought about it before. The idea never hit me. It's very dark out there. There's nothing but a few little stars way overhead and the waves coming in and coming in, over and over and over again. I don't know why I got such a feeling about it. I feel like I'm standing at the edge of the world and these waves are going to keep coming in forever. They'll do it when I'm dead and gone. They'll do it a thousand years from now when the whole world will be so different you couldn't even imagine it, when nobody alive now will even be remembered. Somebody will stand here and these waves will keep coming in and coming in and coming in. I don't know why that got to me so much. I stood there thinking about it. Then finally I went back to the casino to gamble the way I was supposed to.

I don't know if it was because I was standing by the ocean for so long and breathing in the salt air or what, but as soon as I opened the door to the casino I got this smell up my nose which I can't exactly describe. Something like wet metal. But it was sickening to me. Maybe it was my imagination but I thought I was smelling the money. I went in to gamble and the whole time I was there I felt queasy, like this smell was making me nauseous. I figured it was something I ate. But the next day as soon as I went into the casino I smelled it again. I believe I really was smelling the money. I couldn't enjoy gambling any more because of it. It's like the money made me nauseous. That's a very bad condition to be in in Atlantic City. The whole place down there is nothing but money. Money is the whole purpose of everything down there. There is absolutely nothing to it except money. They don't produce anything, they don't do anything, they just move money back and forth, back and forth, and keep raking off the percent that the games are set to give them.

I'm watching this and I'm getting sick. I can't stand the smell. It's like I can feel that money going back and forth and it's making me nauseous all the time. A couple of days later, when the police finally came for me, I was actually relieved to get out of there. I don't say I'd have been relieved if I didn't know this was all a setup and I'd be free in a few hours. I'm not that stupid.

Right on schedule, according to plan, Grenlily sent somebody to bail me out. I got the cash from the safe deposit box, went back to New York, and gave it all to Al Croppe. He says to me, "This will cover our expenses and the law fees Donnie has to pay in New Jersey. After he gets you off and sues the hotel we get our share."

I'm patient. So far he's kept his word. He had Sid General deliver an envelope with a hundred dollars to Brenda right after they got back from the airport. He told her it was from a friend. She didn't want to take it but Sid forced her to. And naturally she used it. She had no choice. When I got back she asked me who was the fat guy in a white suit who gave her the money and what was it all about. I said, "Don't ask me yet. I'll tell you everything when it's settled."

She was glad to have me back. I put the clothes in the suitcases and put them both under the bed. I brought out the silk nightgown I got her in Atlantic City and gave it to her. But it turned into a letdown. She wasn't as happy as I thought she'd be. When I saw that I was glad I hadn't given her the five hundred yet because it proved I had to do it under the right circumstances or the whole thing would be spoiled. I'd feel very bad if I gave her five hundred dollars and she had the same look as when I gave her the silk night-gown. Of course, once I got the twenty-five thousand it would be different. That would throw everything into a different category.

I went back to driving a cab. A couple of times I ran into Dave Winger. He looked bad. I didn't ask him what was happening because I didn't want him to ask me any questions. I was sure he didn't know that I went to Atlantic City but I didn't want to give him the opportunity to ask in case he did find out. Then one day he told me he was going back to Ohio. I wished him luck and I thought I'd never see him again. And I figured that was best for all concerned.

A couple of weeks went by. I had a little money that I kept for myself from all those five hundreds I was supposed to gamble away in Atlantic City. I used it to take Brenda to the movies and a nice dinner. But the main thing I did was I rented a safe deposit box and put my thousand dollars in it. I tied the keys on a string and from then on I kept those two keys around my neck like dog tags in the army.

Finally the court case came up and it goes just like Croppe said it would. We turn around and sue the hotel. It doesn't take long for them to offer a settlement. One day in May Al Croppe gets in touch with me and tells me it's time to go up to Donnie Grenlily's office, sign the papers, and collect our money.

22

I MET AL ON ROOSEVELT, WE GET A CAB AND GO TO
Long Island City which is where Grenlily's
office is. He says to me, "You got something
to carry it in?"

I say, "I thought it'd be a check."

He says, "I don't take checks. This is a
strictly cash business. We'll have to find
you a bag to carry it in."

I'm not worried about that. I'm thinking
of my safe deposit box. That's where I'm
going to put this money. Right on top of the
original thousand. Croppe doesn't know I
have this box. Nobody knows. Not even
Brenda. I got the keys around my neck so

she knows I've got them but she doesn't know what they're for. I told her they're my lucky charm. I'm still deciding what to do with that original thousand but now, with twenty-six thousand, it's a whole different thing.

We get out at this fancy old building. Actually the building is not fancy, just the front of it is. What's going on in Long Island City is that they're taking these old factories and warehouses which used to be built with fancy stone fronts, they're steam cleaning them and converting them to offices. Like in Soho. The whole area was very run down but now all of a sudden it's "in."

We go though the glass doors into this little lobby and get the elevator to the second floor. We find a door which says "Donald H. Grenlily, Counselor-at-Law" and Croppe knocks. A buzzer unlocks the door and we go in. I'm a little surprised at the setup. It's a tiny room with no windows, silver wallpaper, and two metal doors, one opposite the other. It looks weird. Like a science fiction movie. There's nothing in there but a black table with a telephone on it. Al picks up the phone and says, "It's me. Me and Russ." A couple of seconds later the door opens. Originally I pictured Grenlily as a fat, bald guy with a big cigar. I don't know why but that was the picture I had of him. But when I saw that room with the silver wallpaper I didn't know what to expect. Somehow I didn't think a fat guy would have a little room like that. It turns out he's a tall, young guy who probably works out every day. Right there in the office he's got one of those exercise bikes and some weights. It's a very big office but there's hardly any furniture. Wall-to-wall carpet, but all he's got in there besides his bike and the weights at one end is a table with a chair for him, three chairs for visitors, and a filing cabinet. The whole middle of the floor is empty. The really impressive thing, the first thing you notice, besides how big and empty it is, is this huge semicircular window where you can see the Queensborough Bridge and the whole Manhattan skyline.

Al introduces me, we shake hands and sit down. Grenlily has his back to the window but we're facing it and I'm looking at the bridge, the ramps, the cars and trucks going up and down—you can see everything. I'm looking at them and I'm feeling like I've really come up in the world. This is the kind of view rich people get.

Grenlily says to me, "Russ, what's your average daily income?"

I thought he's going to tell me what this money will do for me, how it'll raise my income if I invest it right but I'm not so quick to answer questions. I say, "I don't know but I think today is going to be above average."

He gives me a smile like that's a funny remark and he says, "Do you have an approximate figure?"

I say, "No, I don't."

He says, "Think about it. What would you estimate?"

I estimate only one thing—this guy is a shark. When he asks me questions I get nervous. I came to collect twenty-five thousand dollars, according to an agreement, not to talk about average daily income. I want to sign, get the money, and get out of there. These guys pulled a scam on banks, hotels, and I don't know what else so there's no reason they wouldn't pull one on me. So I'm not going to answer questions. I say, "I can't say exactly how much. It varies from day to day."

He says, "About."

I say, "There's no 'about.' It depends on the season, the weather, the traffic, everything affects it."

He says, "The hotel asked me for a figure and what you just said is what I stated to them because I assumed that would be your answer. But in the absence of any figure from us they said they would use fifty dollars a day. How does that sound to you?"

I said, "What does my income have to do with this?"

He says, "I'll explain that in a minute. Are they wildly off with their fifty dollars a day?"

I don't know what's happening. Should I say it's low or it's high? I'm dealing with lawyers so I know there's an angle but I have no idea what it is. I say, "Sometimes yes and sometimes no."

He says, "Can you give me a better figure?"

I say, "I can't. Especially if I don't know what it's for."

He says, "All right. Let me ask you another question. Are you in any danger of losing your job?"

I say, "No. Why should I be in danger of losing my job?"

He says, "Are you having problems with any of your neighbors? Has anybody insulted you lately?"

I say, "Why are you asking me these questions? Al told me we were coming to sign papers and collect our money."

Grenlily says, "I called Al yesterday and told him the hotel is ready to settle. They made us an offer which they say is their final offer. If we don't take it they'll go to trial. They say they've been burned too often with this scam and they want to stop it. I'm just telling you their point of view, not mine, and I have to tell you honestly so you'll know what's happening and what you're up against. You may find some of this insulting so I remind you that this is the hotel's point of view, not mine. They feel that you are a weak opponent. They feel that if they get you into the witness box they can break you down. They'll keep you in that box for days, weeks, whatever it takes until you make a mistake and contradict yourself. Then they'll pin that check forgery on you and send you to jail. Even if they can't accomplish that, they will drive up the cost of this trial so far beyond any settlement they have to give you that you'll be financially ruined. You'll be in debt for the rest of your life. That will discourage other people from pulling this scam. You're the ideal person for them because your earnings are so low that you can't show much financial loss. Even if you should lose your job it's not a lot of money. So they can settle for very little. Do you follow what I'm saying? I want you to understand what you're up against."

I sat there looking at him. I knew this would happen. In the back of my mind I knew it all along. I came to collect the twenty-five thousand, but, all along, in the back of my mind, I knew that wasn't the kind of thing that happened to me. He's telling me I'm not worth that much money. Other people are but not me. And I knew that all along. If you say what people are worth in dollars, people like me don't count. People like me can't even make that kind of money as a crook.

He says, "Do you want to pursue the case or sign and settle now?"

I stare at him. I can't even talk.

He says, "It's up to you."

I'm choking. I'm afraid of how my voice will sound but I say, "I'll sign now."

Croppe says, "Oh, no. We're not signing. We're not signing anything. These guys don't scare me. I don't sign unless we get the settlement we want. I won't take less than a quarter of a million. And I'll tell you what else—if they try to pull a bluff on me I'll raise the ante. I'll ask for more money."

Grenlily says, "I'm afraid it's not your decision, Al. It's entirely up to Russ. Your signature isn't needed. Legally you aren't involved in this. The hotel, the police, the courts, nobody knows your name. Russ is the one they're after."

Croppe says, "Russ, don't listen to this. The man is trying to scare you. I've pulled this scam a dozen times and it's worked every time. There is nothing to worry about. Don't sign. They've got nothing on us."

Grenlily says, "All I'm doing is stating facts. You gentlemen have to draw your own conclusions. But, as I say, only Russ has to sign. He's the only one with authority in this case."

I say to Al, "You heard what the man said. You say you pulled this scam a dozen times. Now they're tired of it.

They're out to stop it and I'm the one they're going to get. I got to sign."

Al says to me, "You're chicken."

Grenlily says, "I don't know what arrangement you two gentlemen have but you must understand that by signing now you'll get much less than you expected. Their offer is not high. You won't have much money to cover your costs. My people in New Jersey have to be paid, my fee has to be paid, the expense account also has to be covered. Of course, if you reject the settlement and go to trial, the costs will be much higher. We're dealing with a major court case then. And, as in any trial, you risk losing. Since the money for all the fees and expenses was to come from the settlement and there would be no settlement, in fact there would be a risk of you getting no money at all, and since our bills are unpaid, we'd expect some payment immediately plus a guarantee, such as your house, if you own one, that you would be good for the further expenses."

I say, "I'm not going to trial. I'll sign."

Croppe says, "Listen, Russ, this lawyer is scaring you. There ain't gonna be a trial. Don, you go back to Atlantic City and tell them we're calling their bluff. We're not signing. We're fighting all the way."

I say, "I don't know who's bluffing who and I don't care. All I want is to sign and get out."

Croppe says, "Don't be chicken. I have pulled this deal ten, twelve times and nobody ever chickened out on me. Not even Dave Winger. We got a chance for some real money.

There's twenty-five thousand in it for you, Russ. Don't believe that crap about going to jail. Nobody I worked with
ever went to jail. Even if you lost the case all you got to do is
throw yourself on the mercy of the court and they'll never
send you to jail. You're a family man. You're the breadwin-
ner. You can't lose."

I say, "Al, you can't pull the same scam ten or twelve
times. If I'd known you had I'd never have gone along with
it. This man is your lawyer, you hired him, you work with
him, and he's the one who's telling me to sign. I got to go by
that. Just give me the papers and I'll sign."

Al says, "If you sign, you break our agreement. If you do
that, by rights I don't owe you a cent."

I say, "You said you're a man of your word. If you're not,
that's your problem. I can't help what you do."

He says, "But you put me in a bind, Russ. If you sign, we
get no money. Where am I going to get twenty-five thousand dollars to give you? I'm in debt. I laid out a lot of money
for you. I bought plane tickets, I paid for the clothes, I gave
your wife two hundred, for God's sakes."

I start signing papers. At first I was so anxious to get it
over with that I hardly looked at them but then I caught
myself and stopped. I'm in the lion's den there. I started to
read. I don't understand the legal language but I see that the
settlement is for a hundred thousand dollars. I say, "Mr.
Grenlily, this settlement is for a lot of money."

He says, "We had five negotiating sessions in Atlantic
City that I personally attended. I had to stay overnight in
order to prepare. You're paying me by the hour to represent

you and those five days alone amount to thousands of dollars. I have travel expenses, research, New Jersey people who represent you to the New Jersey courts, and a lot more if you want an itemized list. I just hope the hundred thousand covers it all. I'd hate to have to send you a bill."

23

FOR A WHILE I STAYED AWAY FROM THE GREEN LEAF
Tavern because I didn't want to run into Al
Croppe. I went to work, came home, and
stayed home. And I'll admit I was scared.
What scared me was that I'd get a bill from
Grenlily. He could have sent me a bill for
anything he wanted. He could have taken
my furniture, had my salary garnished—
anything—for the rest of my life. When a
guy like that gets you, you can't get away.
Sometimes, when I started my shift at six in
the morning I'd be filling the tank and
watching the sun come up and I'd feel like

taking off and never coming back. I was afraid to go home and see the mail.

When I went back to the Green Leaf I didn't see Al Croppe. It was a long time before I saw him anywhere. When I did he ignored me. That was fine with me. I didn't want to talk to him. But he let people know that he was mad at me for chickening out on him. He didn't say what it was all about but everybody knows what Al Croppe does. That doesn't matter. He makes a lot of money so people respect him. They respect his opinions. When he smears somebody it sticks. But I still go to the Green Leaf. It's on my way home. It's close to the OTB. So what else am I going to do?

I knew what happened in Grenlily's office. I knew what they were doing. It was all part of the scam. It was a performance. They did a con job on me right in front of my eyes and I was watching and knowing they were doing it but there was nothing I could do about it. They never intended to give me money. They must have been laughing at me the whole time. They probably split the hundred thousand, minus something for Sid General. I'm just glad Grenlily never sent me a bill.

After a while things went back to normal. I drive my cab up and down Queens Boulevard—the same business over and over. All I got going for me now is the keys to the safe deposit box with a thousand dollars. It's mine and nobody knows about it. People may look down on me but inside I know something about myself they don't know. I know I'm worth more than they think. I got my thousand dollars. The only thing that bothers me is that the longer I keep it the less valuable it is. I'm watching the news about inflation and there's nothing I can do about that either. I won't invest the money because when the market crashes or the banks go broke you get nothing.

So time goes by. I get older, Brenda gets older, the kids get older, and my money is worth a little less. My shifts are still twelve hours but they feel longer. Five, six, seven years go by. Once they start rolling away like that you can't remember which year it was when things happened.

One day I dropped a passenger in Manhattan and I'm heading back to Queens. I'm on Second Avenue in the Seventies and I stop for a light. All of a sudden I hear a loud bang and I see that a guy who was crossing the street has come over and banged on the hood of my car. He says, "Russ! Hey, Russ! I'd recognize you anywhere."

I'm wondering which of my fares this is because sometimes you make the same call two, three, four times a month and you get to know the customer and some of them like to pretend they think of you as a friend. This guy is very spiffy. He looks like he just came from the tailor or the barber. He says, "Don't tell me you don't remember me. It is Russ, isn't it?"

I almost drop dead. It's Dave Winger.

He opens the door and gets in. I'm not allowed to pick up people on the street but I'm not going to tell him that. I can't believe the way he looks. When I knew him he couldn't afford clothes. I say, "What are you doing here?"

He says, "I have an office on Madison Avenue. I came out

of law school, took the bar exam in New York, and here I am."

I say, "Madison Avenue. That's high rent."

He says, "You wouldn't believe how high." He says, "Russ, how come you're still driving a cab?"

I laugh. It's a fake laugh but it's the best I can do. I can't even think of an answer. We drive along for a few blocks and he's talking and telling me how great things are and I'm pretending that I feel good too.

Then he says, "I've got to get out here but, Russ, it's great seeing you. Let's get together one of these days and have lunch. How's the family?"

He gets out and I swing left and go over the bridge to Queens. I come down under the Els in Queensborough Plaza. That is such a sleazy place. I head down Queens Boulevard. I'm listening to calls coming over the radio.

"Car number one-ninety-two, Al. You get Fourteen-twenty Twenty-first Avenue for nine dollars."

"Car number one-fifty-five, John. Marine Air Terminal. Mr. Bumpers for fourteen dollars."

"Car number sixty-five, Bill, you get Ten-oh-five Ankena Avenue for eight dollars."

All I hear is dollars. I do three, four, maybe nine, ten dollars at a time, Al Croppe does thousands, maybe Dave is doing millions. But it's all dollars. Dollars. That's all anybody does. That's who you are, that's what you are, that's how smart you are. That's life. All of a sudden I realize the dispatcher is calling me on the radio. "Russ. Car number ninety-seven, Russ. Russ, where are you?" I don't know how long he's been calling me. I call back. He says, "Pay attention to the radio!" He gives me a customer in Sunnyside. I pick her up and she has one of those doggie baskets which she hands to me to put in for her. I can see the little dog in there all squinched up. He can hardly move. He's drooling and whining. It's pitiful. She tells me she's going to LaGuardia Airport. I pull out and she starts to talk. She tells me about the dog, how old it is, the pedigree, all the diseases, how much the vet charges. I'm trying to listen. I like to listen to my customers. You meet all kinds of people. But I can't concentrate. I keep remembering when Dave and I would sit and drink beer in the Green Leaf and talk. I remember what he said and what I said. And now I know where he is and where I am.

I get to LaGuardia. The lady pays for the ride with exact money and then starts looking for a tip. She's got a pocketbook as big as a suitcase. She can't find any money in it. All she's got is traveler's checks. She says, "I'm sorry I don't have any cash for you. Do you ever play the lottery?"

I say, "Occasionally."

She says, "Play these numbers—one, ten, eleven, twenty-one, thirty-one, and forty-one. Will you remember that?"

I say yes. On the way home I buy a lottery ticket. I play those numbers. I had a feeling it was just crazy enough that I might get something out of it.

Then I stopped off at the Green Leaf. Max is gone by now. He had a heart attack. The bartender is an ex-cop named Eddie. The place is as greasy as ever. Eddie is not my favorite guy and I don't talk to him much. I sit there with my beer. I finish it and order a second beer. Then I have a third. I didn't make much money that day so I shouldn't be drinking it up but I feel like I need it. And I don't feel like going home. I hang around until 10:30 when they do the lottery on television. Everybody in there plays so they always turn on the station that shows the drawing. They got little Ping-Pong balls with numbers on them blowing around in a glass case. The balls come up one at a time with the winning numbers. I don't have a single one of them.

I finish my beer and go. I decide to check out tomorrow's races at the OTB office. It's open late. Maybe they'll have something that sounds good. At that hour there's nobody in there but drunks and bums. Papers all over the floor. Guys sitting on the floor looking at racing sheets. They all have rotten teeth. They all know each other and they're laughing and coughing. If the office was closed they'd be under a bridge someplace. There's even some women in there.

I look at the charts but I can't concentrate on what I'm doing. Nothing looks good so I head home.

When I come in Brenda is watching television. The kids are out. They're always out now. I don't know where they are and neither does she.

I lay what's left of my money on the kitchen table. She'll take what she needs. If anything's left, that's mine. She knows I had a few beers on the way home but she doesn't complain. She trusts me and I trust her. You got to be able to trust somebody or you'll go out of your mind. She asks me if I ate. I have to stop and think about it. I'm so tired I can't tell if I'm hungry. She makes spaghetti and then sits down with

me and we eat together. I'm looking at the apartment. The
stuffing is coming out of the cushions. Paint is peeling off the
walls.

I'm sitting there with Brenda and I'm so tired we're not
even talking. It's almost midnight and I've been up since 5
A.M. I got to get up at 5 A.M. tomorrow. If I want any sleep I
have to go to bed right now. But I can't do that. That's why
I'm always so tired.

I take the string with the keys off my neck. It's been there
I don't know how long—five, six, seven years. I plunk the
keys down on the table in front of Brenda and I say, "Happy
birthday."

She says, "It ain't my birthday."

I say, "Take 'em for God's sake before I change my mind."

24

A COUPLE OF DAYS GO BY, MAYBE A WEEK, AND where I used to have a pair of keys around my neck, instead I got nothing. And it's the usual thing—you don't know what something means until you don't have it any more. All the time I had that money I never made any plans. I never realized that thousand dollars was my chance in life. Now it's too late. It's gone because, as far as I'm concerned, I would never ask Brenda to give it back.

Meanwhile I'm waiting to see what Brenda does with the money. So far I see nothing. No clothes, no furniture, no steak dinners. Maybe she paid some bills. But she don't say and I don't ask because I don't want it to look like I'm sorry.

Then one night I come home from work and Brenda is sitting at the kitchen table. Just from looking at her I can tell she's waiting for me. She says to me, "Russ, sit down."

I say, "Brenda, when I want to sit down, I'll sit down. If you got something to tell me, I'm right here. I'm listening. What did you do with the money?"

That last part just slipped out because it was on my mind. I didn't mean to ask her that.

She says to me, "I didn't do anything with the money."

I say, "So what do you want to talk about?"

She says, "I want to buy a car."

Well I don't even know how to address that question. We can't afford a car and she should know that. And I'm feeling so low that I don't need to be put in a position where I have to explain it. I say to her, "Brenda, there's a thousand dollars in that box, not a million. You figure insurance and the rest of it and you don't have enough money for a car."

She says, "We could get a car for maybe five, six hundred dollars. Get it painted, put in nice seat covers, buy a CB radio. Then we put signs in the Green Leaf, the cleaner's, the grocer's, everyplace. 'Russ's Car Service.' We'll charge a dollar, maybe a dollar-fifty cheaper than the other car services. People will call me here and I'll give you the messages on the CB. We keep a hundred percent of the fares plus the tips and we'll be way ahead of where we are now."

Well if it was that simple everybody'd be rich. But things don't work that way. And I don't want to hear from Brenda how to operate a car service. I say to her, "You know who you sound like? You sound like Al Croppe. 'Invest a little money and you're a millionaire overnight.' Let me tell you something. The car service is a regulated industry. To operate a car service you need a permit from the city—which costs money. And you also need a special insurance policy which costs thousands of dollars. So you already don't have enough money." And as I'm saying this I'm getting very mad. I'm so mad that I have to go out and take a walk to calm down.

I go up Woodside Avenue to Northern Boulevard and out Northern past the Ronzoni plant. I'm walking and walking and as I'm walking I'm thinking to myself, Why am I so mad? It's not hard to figure out and I'm going to say it straight. I had that key around my neck a long time and in all those years that idea never occurred to me. So what am I supposed to think? That I'm stupid? That I got no ambition? I don't think that's true but what can I say? All I know is I feel like an idiot and that's why I'm mad. But I will say this about myself—I'm not afraid to give credit where credit is due. So I give Brenda full credit.

I go back home and I say to her, "Maybe you got a good idea after all," and I take the thousand dollars and invest in a car. I knew a guy in the used car business who gave me a very good deal. I put in seat covers, nice rugs, and a CB radio. Then I go around to some stores where they know me, put signs in the windows, and I'm in business.

As far as the law that I was telling Brenda about is concerned and the insurance policy and the rest of it, I take the attitude that until somebody bothers me I don't need it. So that means, without the permit and the insurance and the rest of it, and being only one car, I got no overhead. And that means I can be cheaper than anybody else. So pretty soon I'm doing a nice business.

The funny thing is that my clientele reminds me of Dave Winger. It's not just the same kind of people, it's the very same people themselves. For instance, I got the Blitnises as regular customers. The doctors are always giving Harry Blitnis tests. So between the round-trips to the gallbladder doctor and the cardiologist they're good for four to eight rides a month. On top of that, once a week, Wednesday morning, I got a standing order with them for a ride to the Georgia Diner where they get the bus to Atlantic City. They don't tip much but I keep the whole fare instead of just thirty-five percent, so it's still a big improvement.

I don't even have to advertise. Word of mouth does everything for me. These old people got nothing to do but talk and they got nothing to talk about. So whatever's new or a little bit different they talk about over and over until you could turn blue in the face. But for me it's good because they tell each other how nice I am or how nice Brenda is and from that alone I got more business than I can handle.

And Brenda is perfect in this line of work. The clientele love her. She gets on the phone and talks and she's so nice and friendly that she knows them all by name and she knows their whole business. Sometimes I'm tied up with rides for an hour and a half but they say they'll wait for me anyway. Not just because they want to save a dollar and a half on the ride but because they want to talk to Brenda.

So all of a sudden things are a little different in my house. I don't mean I'm rich. You don't get rich from driving one car for one shift. We got a little more money but we're in the same apartment and we got the same furniture. But, for me, it's a lot better than before because I feel different. I'm my own boss. There's no wise guy in the dispatch office who can insult me whenever he's in a bad mood.

From that time on I never heard of Dave Winger again and I'm not sorry because I already knew all about him from what I saw the last time he got in my car.

But I did hear from Al Croppe.

One day I get a call to pick up a customer on Twenty-first Avenue in Long Island City. This is unusual because it's way out of my area. I pull up there and who do I see? Not Al Croppe but his lawyer, Grenlily. He gets in the back seat, makes himself comfortable, and says hello like he expects I'm glad to see him.

I say, "Where do you want to go?"

He says, "Let's stay right here. I want to talk to you, Russ. How are you?"

I say, "I'm fine."

He says, "Russ, I'll come straight to the point. I'm here representing Al Croppe. Now before you say anything let me tell you that Al knows he did you dirty and he knows you've got a right to be angry. Okay? And, what's more, he apologizes. If you give him the chance he'll apologize to your face. Russ, things have happened to Al. He's a different man. If you see him you'll know what I'm talking about. Now I know you're impatient but, please, just give me a little time to explain why I called you."

What can I say? He's sitting in my car. I tell him, "Go ahead. Say what you want."

He says, "I don't have to tell you that Al Croppe was a con man. You also know that Al Croppe ran a lot of scams, not just the one in Atlantic City. And you probably know he made a lot of money. But, Russ, that's all beside the point now. Al can't do it anymore. He's very sick and he needs help. Believe it or not, the kind of help Al needs most is something only you can give him. I know how strange that must sound so let me explain. Russ, Al is hearing the voice of mortality and it makes him nervous. He's done a lot of bad things in his life and now he wants to do something good before it's too late. He hurt you, Russ, he knows that, and he wants to make it up to you. Listen to what he wants to do. Al would like to put his money in your business. Now I want to lay all the cards on the table right from the beginning so let me make this clear—there's something in it for him too. Here's what I mean. All of Al's money is cash. Cash is not legitimate money because it's not registered with the government. There are no taxes paid. So there are things you can't use this money for. He needs to invest his money to make it legitimate. He needs to have it on the books somewhere. Now, he could invest anyplace. He could invest in IBM. But he won't do that because he owes you. He wants to put at least fifty thousand dollars into your business. You remain the owner. You run the business. You become rich. But he gets a legitimate source of income. Al is in my office right now. You don't have to commit yourself to anything. Just come up and talk to him. Listen to what he has to say."

This is crazy. I've been through this with these guys already and I don't trust them. I'm not stupid. But he is talking about fifty thousand dollars so I don't like to just say no without hearing his story. I don't know what to say. I say, "I'm working, Mr. Grenlily. I came here because you called and said you wanted a car."

He says, "I'll pay your hourly rate. No problem. Just come up and talk to the man."

I don't want to do it. Only a sucker gets burned twice. But for fifty thousand dollars, which I know Al Croppe has, I can't just say, "No, forget it. I'm not interested." I have to go up and listen. Even if it's just out of curiosity.

I get out of the car and we go up to the office. First we come to that little silver room with the black telephone. Grenlily opens the inside door and there's the big room with the blue carpet, the view of Manhattan in the semicircular window, the bicycle, the weights, the desk, and the three chairs in front of it. Al is sitting in the middle chair.

I see right away that it's not the same Al. He looks like a very sick man. All dried up and shriveled. The jacket is two sizes too big on him. He gives me this weak smile and holds out his hand like it's hard for him to do that. I take his hand and I'm shocked. It's cold. And not just cold. It's shaking and weak so I feel like just by giving him a normal handshake I'll break his arm. Now, all of a sudden, I have to think that maybe this isn't a scam. And believe me, that doesn't make me happy. I still don't want to be mixed up with these guys.

But now I don't know what to think. I say, "How you doing, Al?"

His voice is low and he talks like he's got no strength. He says, "I'm okay, Russ. I'm grateful to you for coming. I've been wanting to apologize to you."

I say, "Ah, forget it."

He says, "Russ, you're a good man. I want you to do me a favor. Would you do me a favor?"

I say, "What is it?"

He says, "Russ, I don't know what's going to happen to me but I need help. Listen to me. I got cash. A lot of cash. But cash is not legitimate money. It's not listed with the government. I need legitimate money, Russ, so I can get top medical help. Russ, you're also off the books. I know that. Make me your partner. We'll both go legitimate. Fifty thousand dollars. More, if you want. New cars. An office. Air conditioned. Suits. Whatever you want." And as he's talking he gets weaker and weaker until he fades out and shuts his eyes.

What can I say? That I don't want fifty thousand dollars? Of course I want fifty thousand dollars. But I don't trust him. Maybe it's crazy. The man is sitting right in front of me and I can see how sick he is but I don't trust him. And to tell you the truth, I'm still thinking about how he humiliated me and I'd still like to get even with him for that. Not that I would actually do it now. The man is dying. He's apologizing. Offering me money. What else do I want? I should be grateful.

He's got his eyes shut and he says to me, "How 'bout it,

Russ? Fifty thousand. Donnie will draw up the papers."

I don't say anything.

His hand is shaking but he goes into his jacket pocket, pulls out a checkbook and a pen, writes a check, and hands it to me. I'm saying to myself, What is he pulling on me this time? And I'm worried he'll make a fool out of me again. I take the check and it's for fifty thousand dollars. I'm looking at it and as I'm looking at it I get so crazy that I tear it up and I say to him, "Al, how does this scam work? I don't understand it." And as I'm saying it, I'm thinking to myself, How can I talk to him like this? The man is dying.

Al is speechless. I never seen him speechless before. Grenlily doesn't believe it either but Grenlily is a different character. He looks at me like I'm slime. He opens his desk drawer, which I can see is full of money, and he tosses a hundred-dollar bill on the desk and says, "That's your hourly rate. Keep the change and get out of here."

But Al says to me, "Wait a minute. Why do you think this is a scam?" He sits up and, all of a sudden, right in front of me, he starts to turn into the old Al. It's fantastic. The man actually had made himself look smaller. And now, as I'm looking at him, it's like he's filling up with air. I can't believe it. He's not shriveled anymore. His voice is normal. Even the jacket fits him.

To this day I couldn't answer the question he asked me. In fact, I didn't know it was a scam. All I knew is that these guys were offering me fifty thousand dollars again and I knew I was never going to get that kind of money from them or anybody and so I went crazy. That's why I tore up the check. When he sat up and looked normal, that's when I knew it was a scam, not before. If they held out a little longer, maybe I would have gone along with them. I couldn't walk out on a sick man like that. But once I see him sitting there, the old Al, then I know what's happening.

And I've learned a few things myself. So I say to him, "Al, you better think this over. If a dumb guy like me sees it's a scam, everybody's gonna see it. You gotta figure out what you're doing wrong, otherwise you'll get caught."

I pick up the hundred from the desk, pull a ten from my pocket, slap it down, and say, "There's your change." I'm looking right at Grenlily. What I would like to do is say something to him that goes into his heart like a knife. But you know how that is. I can't think of anything. If I do, it'll be a week too late. So I turn around and walk out.

I go downstairs, get in the car, and call Brenda. I say, "That last customer was an hourly rate and he gave me a ninety-dollar tip."

This is like an extra day's pay so naturally she's excited. But I still got one more call to make before I'm finished. I drive over to Ketchem Street and pick up the Blitnises for Harry's doctor's appointment. The two of them get in the car and I say, "You know who I just saw? You remember Al Croppe?"

Mrs. Blitnis says, "Of course I remember Al Croppe. The gentleman from Philadelphia. How could I forget him?"

I say, "The guy is such a con artist you wouldn't believe it."

She says, "What do you mean 'con artist'?"

Harry says, "Never mind. Russ is right. I knew he was a con artist the first minute I saw him. Didn't I say it? Russ, sometimes a con artist can fool you because he's wearing sheep's clothing. But underneath, he's always a leopard. And you know the saying—The leopard does not change his seats."

I drop them off at the doctor's office and head home. On the way, I decide to do something special. I get Chinese take-out and a cold six-pack and bring it home. Me and Brenda sit down, go through the food and the six beers, and we're feeling pretty good.

She says to me, "How were you so sure he was faking?"

I say, "I wasn't sure."

She says, "Then how could you take such a chance to insult him?"

I say, "I had a feeling. It's like a horse race. Sometimes you go with your feeling. Not everything in this world is written on those philosophy cards they got in Paris."

She says, "What philosophy cards in Paris?"

I say, "They got philosophy cards in Paris with sayings on them."

She says, "How do you know about philosophy cards in Paris?"

I say, "I know about a lot of things."

She says, "That's true. In fact, I'm the one who always said that."

I say, "And you were right."

She laughs. So I start to laugh. I just hope we're both laughing for the same reason.